PENGUIN BOOKS

UNEASY MONEY

P. G. Wodehouse was born in Guildford in 1881 and educated at Dulwich College. After working for the Hong Kong and Shanghai Bank for two years, he left to earn his living as a journalist and storywriter, writing the 'By the Way' column in the old *Globe*. He also contributed a series of school stories to a magazine for boys, the *Captain*, in one of which Psmith made his first appearance. Going to America before the First World War, he sold a serial to the *Saturday Evening Post* and for the next twenty-five years almost all his books appeared first in this magazine. He was part author and writer of the lyrics of eighteen musical comedies including *Kissing Time*; he married in 1914 and in 1955 took American citizenship. He wrote over ninety books and his work has won world-wide acclaim, being translated into many languages. *The Times* hailed him as 'a comic genius recognized in his lifetime as a classic and an old master of farce'.

P. G. Wodehouse said: 'I believe there are two ways of writing novels. One is mine, making a sort of musical comedy without music and ignoring real life altogether; the other is going right deep down into life and not caring a damn . . .' He was created a Knight of the British Empire in the New Year's Honours list in 1975. In a BBC interview he said that he had no ambitions left, now that he had been knighted and there was a waxwork of him in Madame Tussaud's. He died on St Valentine's Day in 1975 at the age of ninety-three.

UNEASY MONEY

P. G. Wodehouse

PENGUIN BOOKS

PENGUIN BOOKS

Published by the Penguin Group
Penguin Books Ltd, 27 Wrights Lane, London w8 5tz, England
Viking Penguin, a division of Penguin Books USA Inc.
375 Hudson Street, New York, New York 10014, USA
Penguin Books Australia Ltd, Ringwood, Victoria, Australia
Penguin Books Canada Ltd, 2801 John Street, Markham, Ontario, Canada l3r 1b4
Penguin Books (NZ) Ltd, 182 190 Wairau Road, Auckland 10, New Zealand

Penguin Books Ltd, Registered Offices: Harmondsworth, Middlesex, England

First published by Methuen 1917
Published in Penguin Books 1958
9 10 8

Printed in England by Clays Ltd, St Ives plc
Set in Linotype Granjon

I

In a day in June, at the hour when London moves abroad in quest of lunch, a young man stood at the entrance of the Bandolero Restaurant looking earnestly up Shaftesbury Avenue – a large young man in excellent condition, with a pleasant, good-humoured, brown, clean-cut face. He paid no attention to the stream of humanity that flowed past him. His mouth was set and his eyes wore a serious, almost a wistful expression. He was frowning slightly. One would have said that here was a man with a secret sorrow.

William FitzWilliam Delamere Chalmers, Lord Dawlish, had no secret sorrow. All that he was thinking of at that moment was the best method of laying a golf ball dead in front of the Palace Theatre. It was his habit to pass the time in mental golf when Claire Fenwick was late in keeping her appointments with him. On one occasion she had kept him waiting so long that he had been able to do nine holes, starting at the Savoy Grill and finishing up near Hammersmith. His was a simple mind, able to amuse itself with simple things.

As he stood there, gazing into the middle distance, an individual of dishevelled aspect sidled up, a vagrant of almost the maximum seediness, from whose midriff there protruded a trayful of a strange welter of collar-studs, shoe-laces, rubber rings, buttonhooks, and dying roosters. For some minutes he had been eyeing his lordship appraisingly from the edge of the kerb, and now, secure in the fact that there seemed to be no policeman in the immediate vicinity, he anchored himself in front of him and observed that he had a wife and four children at home, all starving.

This sort of thing was always happening to Lord Dawlish. There was something about him, some atmosphere of unaffected kindliness, that invited it.

In these days when everything, from the shape of a man's hat to his method of dealing with asparagus, is supposed to be an index to character, it is possible to form some estimate of Lord Dawlish from the fact that his vigil in front of the Bandolero had been expensive even before the advent of the Benedict with the studs and laces. In London, as in New York, there are spots where it is unsafe for a man of yielding disposition to stand still, and the corner of Shaftesbury Avenue and Piccadilly Circus is one of them. Scrubby, impecunious men drift to and fro there, waiting for the gods to provide something easy; and the prudent man, conscious of the possession of loose change, whizzes through the danger zone at his best speed, 'like one that on a lonesome road doth walk in fear and dread, and having once turned round walks on, and turns no more his head, because he knows a frightful fiend doth close behind him tread.' In the seven minutes he had been waiting two frightful fiends closed in on Lord Dawlish, requesting loans of five shillings till Wednesday week and Saturday week respectively, and he had parted with the money without a murmur.

A further clue to his character is supplied by the fact that both these needy persons seemed to know him intimately, and that each called him Bill. All Lord Dawlish's friends called him Bill, and he had a catholic list of them, ranging from men whose names were in 'Debrett' to men whose names were on the notice boards of obscure clubs in connexion with the non-payment of dues. He was the sort of man one instinctively calls Bill.

The anti-race-suicide enthusiast with the rubber rings did not call Lord Dawlish Bill, but otherwise his manner was intimate. His lordship's gaze being a little slow in returning from the middle distance – for it was not a matter to be decided carelessly and without thought, this problem of carrying the length of Shaftesbury Avenue with a single brassy shot – he repeated the gossip from the home. Lord Dawlish regarded him thoughtfully.

'It could be done,' he said, 'but you'd want a bit of pull on it. I'm sorry; I didn't catch what you said.'

The other obliged with his remark for the third time, with increased pathos, for constant repetition was making him almost believe it himself.

'Four starving children?'

'Four, guv'nor, so help me!'

'I suppose you don't get much time for golf then, what?' said Lord Dawlish, sympathetically.

It was precisely three days, said the man, mournfully inflating a dying rooster, since his offspring had tasted bread.

This did not touch Lord Dawlish deeply. He was not very fond of bread. But it seemed to be troubling the poor fellow with the studs a great deal, so, realizing that tastes differ and that there is no accounting for them, he looked at him commiseratingly.

'Of course, if they like bread, that makes it rather rotten, doesn't it? What are you going to do about it?'

'Buy a dying rooster, guv'nor,' he advised. 'Causes great fun and laughter.'

Lord Dawlish eyed the strange fowl without enthusiasm.

'No,' he said, with a slight shudder.

There was a pause. The situation had the appearance of being at a deadlock.

'I'll tell you what,' said Lord Dawlish, with the air of one who, having pondered, has been rewarded with a great idea: 'the fact is, I really don't want to buy anything. You seem by bad luck to be stocked up with just the sort of things I wouldn't be seen dead in a ditch with. I can't stand rubber rings, never could. I'm not really keen on buttonhooks. And I don't want to hurt your feelings, but I think that squeaking bird of yours is about the beastliest thing I ever met. So suppose I give you a shilling and call it square, what?'

'Gawd bless yer, guv'nor.'

'Not at all. You'll be able to get those children of yours some bread – I expect you can get a lot of bread for a shilling. Do they really like it? Rum kids!'

And having concluded this delicate financial deal Lord Dawlish turned, the movement bringing him face to face with a tall girl in white.

During the business talk which had just come to an end this girl had been making her way up the side street which forms a short cut between Coventry Street and the Bandolero, and several admirers of feminine beauty who happened to be using the same route had almost dislocated their necks looking after her. She was a strikingly handsome girl. She was tall and willowy. Her eyes, shaded by her hat, were large and grey. Her nose was small and straight, her mouth, though somewhat hard, admirably shaped, and she carried herself magnificently. One cannot blame the policeman on duty in Leicester Square for remarking to a cabman as she passed that he envied the bloke that that was going to meet.

Bill Dawlish was this fortunate bloke, but, from the look of him as he caught sight of her, one would have said that he did not appreciate his luck. The fact of the matter was that he had only just finished giving the father of the family his shilling, and he was afraid that Claire had seen him doing it. For Claire, dear girl, was apt to be unreasonable about these little generosities of his. He cast a furtive glance behind him in the hope that the disseminator of expiring roosters had vanished, but the man was still at his elbow. Worse, he faced them, and in a hoarse but carrying voice he was instructing Heaven to bless his benefactor.

'Halloa, Claire darling!' said Lord Dawlish, with a sort of sheepish breeziness. 'Here you are.'

Claire was looking after the stud merchant, as, grasping his wealth, he scuttled up the avenue.

'Only a bob,' his lordship hastened to say. 'Rather a sad case, don't you know. Squads of children at home demanding bread. Didn't want much else, apparently, but were frightfully keen on bread.'

'He has just gone into a public-house.'

'He may have gone to telephone or something, what?'

'I wish,' said Claire, fretfully, leading the way down the grill-room stairs, 'that you wouldn't let all London sponge on you like this. I keep telling you not to. I should have thought that if any one needed to keep what little money he has got it was you.'

Certainly Lord Dawlish would have been more prudent not to have parted with even eleven shillings, for he was not a rich man. Indeed, with the single exception of the Earl of Wetherby,

8

whose finances were so irregular that he could not be said to possess an income at all, he was the poorest man of his rank in the British Isles.

It was in the days of the Regency that the Dawlish coffers first began to show signs of cracking under the strain, in the era of the then celebrated Beau Dawlish. Nor were his successors backward in the spending art. A breezy disregard for the preservation of the pence was a family trait. Bill was at Cambridge when his predecessor in the title, his Uncle Philip, was performing the concluding exercises of the dissipation of the Dawlish doubloons, a feat which he achieved so neatly that when he died there was just enough cash to pay the doctors, and no more. Bill found himself the possessor of that most ironical thing, a moneyless title. He was then twenty-three.

Until six months before, when he had become engaged to Claire Fenwick, he had found nothing to quarrel with in his lot. He was not the type to waste time in vain regrets. His tastes were simple. As long as he could afford to belong to one or two golf clubs and have something over for those small loans which, in certain of the numerous circles in which he moved, were the inevitable concomitant of popularity, he was satisfied. And this modest ambition had been realized for him by a group of what he was accustomed to refer to as decent old bucks, who had installed him as secretary of that aristocratic and exclusive club, Brown's in St James Street, at an annual salary of four hundred pounds. With that wealth, added to free lodging at one of the best clubs in London, perfect health, a steadily-diminishing golf handicap, and a host of friends in every walk of life, Bill had felt that it would be absurd not to be happy and contented.

But Claire had made a difference. There was no question of that. In the first place, she resolutely declined to marry him on four hundred pounds a year. She scoffed at four hundred pounds a year. To hear her talk, you would have supposed that she had been brought up from the cradle to look on four hundred pounds a year as small change to be disposed of in tips and cab fares. That in itself would have been enough to sow doubts in Bill's mind as to whether he had really got all the money that a reasonable man needed; and Claire saw to it that these doubts sprouted, by confining her conversation on the occasions of their meeting almost entirely to the great theme of money, with its minor sub-divisions of How to get it, Why don't you get it? and I'm sick and tired of not having it.

She developed this theme to-day, not only on the stairs leading to the grillroom, but even after they had seated themselves at their table. It was a relief to Bill when the arrival of the waiter with food caused a break in the conversation and enabled him adroitly to change the subject.

'What have you been doing this morning?' he asked.

'I went to see Maginnis at the theatre.'

'Oh!'

'I had a wire from him asking me to call. They want me to call. They want me to take up Claudia Winslow's part in the number one company.'

'That's good.'

'Why?'

'Well – er – what I mean – well, isn't it? What I mean is, leading part, and so forth.'

'In a touring company?'

'Yes, I see what you mean,' said Lord Dawlish, who didn't at all. He thought rather highly of the number one companies that hailed from the theatre of which Mr Maginnis was proprietor.

'And anyhow, I ought to have had the part in the first place instead of when the tour's half over. They are at Southampton this week. He wants me to join them there and go on to Portsmouth with them.'

'You'll like Portsmouth.'

'Why?'

'Well – er – good links quite near.'

'You know I don't play golf.'

'Nor do you. I was forgetting. Still, it's quite a jolly place.'

'It's a horrible place. I loathe it. I've half a mind not to go.'

'Oh, I don't know.'

'What do you mean?'

Lord Dawlish was feeling a little sorry for himself. Whatever he said seemed to be the wrong thing. This evidently was one of the days on which Claire was not so sweet-tempered as on some other days. It crossed his mind that of late these irritable moods of hers had grown more frequent. It was not her fault, poor girl! he told himself. She had rather a rotten time.

It was always Lord Dawlish's habit on these occasions to make this excuse for Claire. It was such a satisfactory excuse. It covered everything. But, as a matter of fact, the rather rotten time which she was having was not such a very rotten one. Reducing it to its simplest terms, and forgetting for the moment that she was an extraordinarily beautiful girl – which his lordship found it impossible to do – all that it amounted to was that, her mother having but a small income, and existence in the West Kensington flat being consequently a trifle dull for one with a taste for the luxuries of life, Claire had gone on the stage. By birth she belonged to a class of which the female members are seldom called upon to earn money at all, and that was one count of her grievance against Fate. Another was that she had not done as well on the stage as she had expected to do. When she became engaged to Bill she had reached a point where she could obtain without difficulty good parts in the touring companies of London successes, but beyond that it seemed it was impossible for her to soar. It was not, perhaps, a very exhilarating life, but, except to the eyes of love, there was nothing tragic about it. It was the cumulative effect of having a mother in reduced circumstances and grumbling about it, of being compelled to work and grumbling about that, and of achieving in her work only a semi-success and grumbling about that also, that – backed by her looks – enabled Claire to give quite a number of people, and Bill Dawlish in particular, the impression that she was a modern martyr, only sustained by her indomitable courage.

So Bill, being requested in a peevish voice to explain what he meant by saying, 'Oh, I don't know,' condoned the peevishness. He then bent his mind to the task of trying to ascertain what he had meant.

'Well,' he said, 'what I mean is, if you don't show up won't it be rather a jar for old friend Maginnis? Won't he be apt to foam at the mouth a bit and stop giving you parts in his companies?'

'I'm sick of trying to please Maginnis. What's the good? He never gives me a chance in London. I'm sick of being always on tour. I'm sick of everything.'

'It's the heat,' said Lord Dawlish, most injudiciously.

'It isn't the heat. It's you!'

'Me? What have I done?'

'It's what you've not done. Why can't you exert yourself and make some money?'

Lord Dawlish groaned a silent groan. By a devious route, but with unfailing precision, they had come homing back to the same old subject.

'We have been engaged for six months, and there seems about as much chance of our ever getting married as of – I can't think of anything unlikely enough. We shall go on like this till we're dead.'

'But, my dear girl!'

'I wish you wouldn't talk to me as if you were my grandfather. What were you going to say?'

'Only that we can get married this afternoon if you'll say the word.'

'Oh, don't let us go into all that again! I'm not going to marry on four hundred a year and spend the rest of my life in a pokey little flat on the edge of London. Why can't you make more money?'

'I did have a dash at it, you know. I waylaid old Bodger – Colonel Bodger, on the committee of the club, you know – and suggested over a whisky-and-soda that the management of Brown's would be behaving like sportsmen if they bumped my salary up a bit, and the old boy nearly strangled himself trying to suck down Scotch and laugh at the same time. I give you my word, he nearly expired on the smoking-room floor. When he came to he said that he wished I wouldn't spring my good things on him so suddenly, as he had a weak heart. He said they were only paying me my present salary because they liked me so much. You know, it was decent of the old boy to say that.'

'What is the good of being liked by the men in your club if you won't make any use of it?'

'How do you mean?'

'There are endless things you could do. You could have got Mr Breitstein elected at Brown's if you had liked. They wouldn't have dreamed of blackballing any one proposed by a popular man like you, and Mr Breitstein asked you personally to use your influence – you told me so.'

'But, my dear girl – I mean my darling – Breitstein! He's the limit! He's the worst bounder in London.'

'He's also one of the richest men in London. He would have done anything for you. And you let him go! You insulted him!'

'Insulted him?'

'Didn't you send him an admission ticket to the Zoo?'

'Oh, well, yes, I did do that. He thanked me and went the following Sunday. Amazing how these rich Johnnies love getting something for nothing. There was that old American I met down at Marvis Bay last year –'

'You threw away a wonderful chance of making all sorts of money. Why, a single tip from Mr Breitstein would have made your fortune.'

'But, Claire, you know, there are some things – what I mean is, if they like me at Brown's, it's awfully decent of them and all that, but I couldn't take advantage of it to plant a fellow like Breitstein on them. It wouldn't be playing the game.'

'Oh, nonsense!'

Lord Dawlish looked unhappy, but said nothing. This matter of Mr Breitstein had been touched upon by Claire in previous conversations, and it was a subject for which he had little liking. Experience had taught him that none of the arguments which seemed so conclusive to him – to wit, that the financier had on two occasions only just escaped imprisonment for fraud, and, what was worse, made a noise when he drank soup, like water running out of a bathtub – had the least effect upon her. The only thing to do when Mr Breitstein came up in the course of chitchat over the festive board was to stay quiet until he blew over.

'That old American you met at Marvis Bay,' said Claire, her

memory flitting back to the remark which she had interrupted; 'well, there's another case. You could easily have got him to do something for you.'

'Claire, really!' said his goaded lordship, protestingly. 'How on earth? I only met the man on the links.'

'But you were very nice to him. You told me yourself that you spent hours helping him to get rid of his slice, whatever that is.'

'We happened to be the only two down there at the time, so I was as civil as I could manage. If you're marooned at a Cornish seaside resort out of the season with a man, you can't spend your time dodging him. And this man had a slice that fascinated me. I felt at the time that it was my mission in life to cure him, so I had a dash at it. But I don't see how on the strength of that I could expect the old boy to adopt me. He probably forgot my existence after I had left.'

'You said you met him in London a month or two afterwards, and he hadn't forgotten you.'

'Well, yes, that's true. He was walking up the Haymarket and I was walking down. I caught his eye, and he nodded and passed on. I don't see how I could construe that into an invitation to go and sit on his lap and help myself out of his pockets.'

'You couldn't expect him to go out of his way to help you; but probably if you had gone to him he would have done something.'

'You haven't the pleasure of Mr Ira Nutcombe's acquaintance, Claire, or you wouldn't talk like that. He wasn't the sort of man you could get things out of. He didn't even tip the caddie. Besides, can't you see what I mean? I couldn't trade on a chance acquaintance of the golf links to –'

'That is just what I complain of in you. You're too diffident.'

'It isn't diffidence exactly. Talking of old Nutcombe, I was speaking to Gates again the other night. He was telling me about America. There's a lot of money to be made over there, you know, and the committee owes me a holiday. They would give me a few weeks off any time I liked.

'What do you say? Shall I pop over and have a look round?

I might happen to drop into something. Gates was telling me about fellows he knew who had dropped into things in New York.'

'What's the good of putting yourself to all the trouble and expense of going to America? You can easily make all you want in London if you will only try. It isn't as if you had no chances. You have more chances than almost any man in town. With your title you could get all the directorships in the City that you wanted.'

'Well, the fact is, this business of taking directorships has never quite appealed to me. I don't know anything about the game, and I should probably run up against some wildcat company. I can't say I like the directorship wheeze much. It's the idea of knowing that one's name would be being used as a bait. Every time I saw it on a prospectus I should feel like a trout fly.'

Claire bit her lip.

'It's so exasperating!' she broke out. 'When I first told my friends that I was engaged to Lord Dawlish they were tremendously impressed. They took it for granted that you must have lots of money. Now I have to keep explaining to them that the reason we don't get married is that we can't afford to. I'm almost as badly off as poor Polly Davis who was in the Heavenly Waltz Company with me when she married that man, Lord Wetherby. A man with a title has no right not to have money. It makes the whole thing farcical.

'If I were in your place I should have tried a hundred things by now, but you always have some silly objection. Why couldn't you, for instance, have taken on the agency of that what-d'you-call-it car?'

'What I called it would have been nothing to what the poor devils who bought it would have called it.'

'You could have sold hundreds of them, and the company would have given you any commission you asked. You know just the sort of people they wanted to get in touch with.'

'But, darling, how could I? Planting Breitstein on the club would have been nothing compared with sowing these horrors about London. I couldn't go about the place sticking my pals

with a car which, I give you my honest word, was stuck together with chewing-gum and tied up with string.'

'Why not? It would be their fault if they bought a car that
wasn't any good. Why should you have to worry once you
had it sold?'

It was not Lord Dawlish's lucky afternoon. All through
lunch he had been saying the wrong thing, and now he put
the coping-stone on his misdeeds. Of all the ways in which he
could have answered Claire's question he chose the worst.

'Er – well,' he said, '*noblesse oblige*, don't you know, what?'

For a moment Claire did not speak. Then she looked at her
watch and got up.

'I must be going,' she said, coldly.

'But you haven't had your coffee yet.'

'I don't want any coffee.'

'What's the matter, dear?'

'Nothing is the matter. I have to go home and pack. I'm
going to Southampton this afternoon.'

She began to move towards the door. Lord Dawlish, anxious
to follow, was detained by the fact that he had not yet paid the
bill. The production and settling of this took time, and when
finally he turned in search of Claire she was nowhere visible.

Bounding upstairs on the swift feet of love, he reached the
street. She had gone.

2

A GREY sadness surged over Bill Dawlish. The sun hid itself
behind a cloud, the sky took on a leaden hue, and a chill wind
blew through the world. He scanned Shaftesbury Avenue with
a jaundiced eye, and thought that he had never seen a beastlier
thoroughfare. Piccadilly, however, into which he shortly dragged himself, was even worse. It was full of men and women
and other depressing things.

He pitied himself profoundly. It was a rotten world to live
in, this, where a fellow couldn't say *noblesse oblige* without
upsetting the universe. Why shouldn't a fellow say *noblesse*

oblige? Why –? At this juncture Lord Dawlish walked into a lamp-post.

The shock changed his mood. Gloom still obsessed him, but blended now with remorse. He began to look at the matter from Claire's viewpoint, and his pity switched from himself to her. In the first place, the poor girl had rather a rotten time. Could she be blamed for wanting him to make money? No. Yet whenever she made suggestions as to how the thing was to be done, he snubbed her by saying *noblesse oblige*. Naturally a refined and sensitive young girl objected to having things like *noblesse oblige* said to her. Where was the sense in saying *noblesse oblige?* Such a confoundedly silly thing to say. Only a perfect ass would spend his time rushing about the place saying *noblesse oblige* to people.

'By Jove!' Lord Dawlish stopped in his stride. He disentangled himself from a pedestrian who had rammed him on the back. 'I'll do it!'

He hailed a passing taxi and directed the driver to make for the Pen and Ink Club.

The decision at which Bill had arrived with such dramatic suddenness in the middle of Piccadilly was the same at which some centuries earlier Columbus had arrived in the privacy of his home.

'Hang it!' said Bill to himself in the cab, 'I'll go to America!' The exact words probably which Columbus had used, talking the thing over with his wife.

Bill's knowledge of the great republic across the sea was at this period of his life a little sketchy. He knew that there had been unpleasantness between England and the United States in seventeen-something and again in eighteen-something, but that things had eventually been straightened out by Miss Edna May and her fellow missionaries of the Belle of New York Company, since which time there had been no more trouble. Of American cocktails he had a fair working knowledge, and he appreciated ragtime. But of the other great American institutions he was completely ignorant.

He was on his way now to see Gates. Gates was a comparatively recent addition to his list of friends, a New York newspaperman who had come to England a few months before to act as his paper's London correspondent. He was generally to be found at the Pen and Ink Club, an institution affiliated with the New York Players, of which he was a member.

Gates was in. He had just finished lunch.

'What's the trouble, Bill?' he inquired, when he had deposited his lordship in a corner of the reading-room, which he had selected because silence was compulsory there, thus rendering it possible for two men to hear each other speak. 'What brings you charging in here looking like the Soul's Awakening?'

'I've had an idea, old man.'

'Proceed. Continue.'

'Oh! Well, you remember what you were saying about America?'

'What was I saying about America?'

'The other day, don't you remember? What a lot of money there was to be made there and so forth.'

'Well?'

'I'm going there.'

'To America?'

'Yes.'

'To make money?'

'Rather.'

Gates nodded – sadly, it seemed to Bill. He was rather a melancholy young man, with a long face not unlike a pessimistic horse.

'Gosh!' he said.

Bill felt a little damped. By no mental juggling could he construe 'Gosh!' into an expression of enthusiastic approbation.

Gates looked at Bill curiously. 'What's the idea?' he said. 'I could have understood it if you had told me that you were going to New York for pleasure, instructing your man Willoughby to see that the trunks were jolly well packed and wiring to the skipper of your yacht to meet you at Liverpool. But you seem to have sordid motives. You talk about making money. What do you want with more money?'

'Why, I'm devilish hard up.'

'Tenantry a bit slack with the rent?' said Gates sympathetically.

Bill laughed.

'My dear chap, I don't know what on earth you're talking about. How much money do you think I've got? Four hundred pounds a year, and no prospect of ever making more unless I sweat for it.'

'What! I always thought you were rolling in money.'

'What gave you that idea?'

'You have a prosperous look. It's a funny thing about England. I've known you four months, and I know men who know you; but I've never heard a word about your finances. In New York we all wear labels, stating our incomes and prospects in clear lettering. Well, if it's like that it's different, of course. There certainly is more money to be made in America than here. I don't quite see what you think you're going to do when you get there, but that's up to you.

'There's no harm in giving the city a trial. Anyway, I can give you a letter or two that might help.'

'That's awfully good of you.'

'You won't mind my alluding to you as my friend William Smith?'

'William Smith?'

'You can't travel under your own name if you are really serious about getting a job. Mind you, if my letters lead to anything it will probably be a situation as an earnest bill-clerk or an effervescent office-boy, for Rockefeller and Carnegie and that lot have swiped all the soft jobs. But if you go over as Lord Dawlish you won't even get that. Lords are popular socially in America, but are not used to any great extent in the office. If you try to break in under your right name you'll get the glad hand and be asked to stay here and there and play a good deal of golf and dance quite a lot, but you won't get a job. A gentle smile will greet all your pleadings that you be allowed to come in and save the firm.'

'I see.'

'We may look on Smith as a necessity.'

'Do you know, I'm not frightfully keen on the name Smith. Wouldn't something else do?'

'Sure. We aim to please. How would Jones suit you?'

'The trouble is, you know, that if I took a name I wasn't used to I might forget it.'

'If you've the sort of mind that would forget Jones I doubt if ever you'll be a captain of industry.'

'Why not Chalmers?'

'You think it easier to memorize than Jones?'

'It used to be my name, you see, before I got the title.'

'I see. All right. Chalmers then. When do you think of starting?'

'To-morrow.'

'You aren't losing much time. By the way, as you're going to New York you might as well use my flat.'

'It's awfully good of you.'

'Not a bit. You would be doing me a favour. I had to leave at a moment's notice, and I want to know what's been happening to the place. I left some Japanese prints there, and my favourite nightmare is that someone has broken in and sneaked them. Write down the address – Forty-blank East Twenty-seventh Street. I'll send you the key to Brown's to-night with those letters.'

Bill walked up the Strand, glowing with energy. He made his way to Cockspur Street to buy his ticket for New York. This done, he set out to Brown's to arrange with the committee the details of his departure.

He reached Brown's at twenty minutes past two and left it again at twenty-three minutes past; for, directly he entered, the hall porter had handed him a telephone message. The telephone attendants at London clubs are masters of suggestive brevity. The one in the basement of Brown's had written on Bill's slip of paper the words: '1 p.m. Will Lord Dawlish as soon as possible call upon Mr Gerald Nichols at his office?' To this was appended a message consisting of two words: 'Good news.'

It was stimulating. The probability was that all Jerry Nichols wanted to tell him was that he had received stable information about some horse or had been given a box for the Empire, but for all that it was stimulating.

Bill looked at his watch. He could spare half an hour. He set out at once for the offices of the eminent law firm of Nichols, Nichols, Nichols, and Nichols, of which aggregation of Nicholses his friend Jerry was the last and smallest.

3

On a west-bound omnibus Claire Fenwick sat and raged silently in the June sunshine. She was furious. What right had Lord Dawlish to look down his nose and murmur *'Noblesse oblige'* when she asked him a question, as if she had suggested that he should commit some crime? It was the patronizing way he had said it that infuriated her, as if he were a superior being of some kind, governed by codes which she could not be expected to understand. Everybody nowadays did the sort of things she suggested, so what was the good of looking shocked and saying *'Noblesse oblige'*?

The omnibus rolled on towards West Kensington. Claire hated the place with the bitter hate of one who had read society novels, and yearned for Grosvenor Square and butlers and a general atmosphere of soft cushions and pink-shaded lights and maids to do one's hair. She hated the cheap furniture of the little parlour, the penetrating contralto of the cook singing hymns in the kitchen, and the ubiquitousness of her small brother. He was only ten, and small for his age, yet he appeared to have the power of being in two rooms at the same time while making a nerve-racking noise in another.

It was Percy who greeted her to-day as she entered the flat.

'Halloa, Claire! I say, Claire, there's a letter for you. It came by the second post. I say, Claire, it's got an American stamp on it. Can I have it, Claire? I haven't got one in my collection.'

His sister regarded him broodingly. 'For goodness' sake don't bellow like that!' she said. 'Of course, you can have the stamp. I don't want it. Where is the letter?'

Claire took the envelope from him, extracted the letter, and handed back the envelope. Percy vanished into the dining-room with a shattering squeal of pleasure.

A voice spoke from behind a half-opened door –

'Is that you, Claire?'

'Yes, mother; I've come back to pack. They want me to go to Southampton to-night to take up Claudia Winslow's part.'

'What train are you catching?'

'The three-fifteen.'

'You will have to hurry.'

'I'm going to hurry,' said Claire, clenching her fists as two simultaneous bursts of song, in different keys and varying tempos, proceeded from the dining-room and kitchen. A girl has to be in a sunnier mood than she was to bear up without wincing under the infliction of a duet consisting of the Rock of Ages and Waiting for the Robert E. Lee. Assuredly Claire proposed to hurry. She meant to get her packing done in record time and escape from this place. She went into her bedroom and began to throw things untidily into her trunk. She had put the letter in her pocket against a more favourable time for perusal. A glance had told her that it was from her friend Polly, Countess of Wetherby: that Polly Davis of whom she had spoken to Lord Dawlish. Polly Davis, now married for better or for worse to that curious invertebrate person, Algie Wetherby, was the only real friend Claire had made on the stage. A sort of shivering gentility had kept her aloof from the rest of her fellow-workers, but it took more than a shivering gentility to stave off Polly.

Claire had passed through the various stages of intimacy with her, until on the occasion of Polly's marriage she had acted as her bridesmaid.

It was a long letter, too long to be read until she was at leisure, and written in a straggling hand that made reading difficult. She was mildly surprised that Polly should have written her, for she had been back in America a year or more now, and this was her first letter. Polly had a warm heart and did not forget her friends, but she was not a good correspondent.

The need of getting her things ready at once drove the letter from Claire's mind. She was in the train on her way to Southampton before she remembered its existence.

It was dated from New York.

MY DEAR OLD CLAIRE, – Is this really my first letter to you? Isn't that awful! Gee! A lot's happened since I saw you last. I must tell you first about my hit. Some hit! Claire, old girl, I own New York. I daren't tell you what my salary is. You'd faint.

I'm doing barefoot dancing. You know the sort of stuff. I started it in vaudeville, and went so big that my agent shifted me to the restaurants, and they have to call out the police reserves to handle the crowd. You can't get a table at Reigelheimer's, which is my pitch, unless you tip the head waiter a small fortune and promise to mail him your clothes when you get home. I dance during supper with nothing on my feet and not much anywhere else, and it takes three vans to carry my salary to the bank.

Of course, it's the title that does it: 'Lady Pauline Wetherby!' Algie says it oughtn't to be that, because I'm not the daughter of a duke, but I don't worry about that. It looks good, and that's all that matters. You can't get away from the title. I was born in Carbondale, Illinois, but that doesn't matter – I'm an English countess, doing barefoot dancing to work off the mortgage on the ancestral castle, and they eat me. Take it from me, Claire, I'm a riot.

Well, that's that. What I am really writing about is to tell you that you have got to come over here. I've taken a house at Brookport, on Long Island, for the summer. You can stay with me till the fall, and then I can easily get you a good job in New York. I have some pull these days, believe me. Not that you'll need my help. The managers have only got to see you and they'll all want you. I showed one of them that photograph you gave me, and he went up in the air. They pay twice as big salaries over here, you know, as in England, so come by the next boat.

Claire, darling, you must come. I'm wretched. Algie has got my goat the worst way. If you don't know what that means it means that he's behaving like a perfect pig. I hardly know where to begin. Well, it was this way: directly I made my hit my press agent, a real bright man named Sherriff, got busy, of course. Interviews, you know, and Advice to Young Girls in the evening papers, and How I preserve my beauty, and all that sort of thing. Well, one thing he made me do was to buy a snake and a monkey. Roscoe

Sherriff is crazy about animals as aids to advertisement. He says an animal story is the thing he does best. So I bought them.

Algie kicked from the first. I ought to tell you that since we left England he has taken up painting footling little pictures, and has got the artistic temperament badly. All his life he's been starting some new fool thing. When I first met him he prided himself on having the finest collection of photographs of race-horses in England. Then he got a craze for model engines. After that he used to work the piano player till I nearly went crazy. And now it's pictures.

I don't mind his painting. It gives him something to do and keeps him out of mischief. He has a studio down in Washington Square, and is perfectly happy messing about there all day.

Everything would be fine if he didn't think it necessary to tack on the artistic temperament to his painting. He's developed the idea that he has nerves and everything upsets them.

Things came to a head this morning at breakfast. Clarence, my snake, has the cutest way of climbing up the leg of the table and looking at you pleadingly in the hope that you will give him soft-boiled egg, which he adores. He did it this morning, and no sooner had his head appeared above the table than Algie, with a kind of sharp wail, struck him a violent blow on the nose with a teaspoon. Then he turned to me, very pale, and said: 'Pauline, this must end! The time has come to speak up. A nervous, highly-strung man like myself should not, and must not, be called upon to live in a house where he is constantly meeting snakes and monkeys without warning. Choose between me and – '

We had got as far as this when Eustace, the monkey, who I didn't know was in the room at all, suddenly sprang on to his back. He is very fond of Algie.

Would you believe it? Algie walked straight out of the house, still holding the teaspoon, and has not returned. Later in the day he called me up on the phone and said that, though he realized that a man's place was the home, he declined to cross the threshold again until I had got rid of Eustace and Clarence. I tried to reason with him. I told him that he ought to think himself lucky it wasn't anything worse than a monkey and a snake, for the last person Roscoe Sherriff handled, an emotional actress named Devenish, had to keep a young puma. But he wouldn't listen, and the end of it was that he rang off and I have not seen or heard of him since.

I am broken-hearted. I won't give in, but I am having an awful time. So, dearest Claire, do come over and help me. If you could possibly sail by the *Atlantic*, leaving Southampton on the twenty-fourth of this month, you would meet a friend of mine whom I think you would like. His name is Dudley Pickering, and he made a fortune in automobiles. I expect you have heard of the Pickering automobiles?

Darling Claire, do come, or I know I shall weaken and yield to Algie's outrageous demands, for, though I would like to hit him with a brick, I love him dearly.

Your affectionate

POLLY WETHERBY

Claire sank back against the cushioned seat and her eyes filled with tears of disappointment. Of all the things which would have chimed in with her discontented mood at that moment a sudden flight to America was the most alluring. Only one consideration held her back – she had not the money for her fare.

Polly might have thought of that, she reflected, bitterly. She took the letter up again and saw that on the last page there was a postscript –

PS. – I don't know how you are fixed for money, old girl, but if things are the same with you as in the old days you can't be rolling. So I have paid for a passage for you with the liner people this side, and they have cabled their English office, so you can sail whenever you want to. Come right over.

An hour later the manager of the Southampton branch of the White Star Line was dazzled by an apparition, a beautiful girl who burst in upon him with flushed face and shining eyes, demanding a berth on the steamship *Atlantic* and talking about a Lady Wetherby. Ten minutes later, her passage secured, Claire was walking to the local theatre to inform those in charge of the destinies of The Girl and the Artist number one company that they must look elsewhere for a substitute for Miss Claudia Winslow. Then she went back to her hotel to write a letter home, notifying her mother of her plans.

She looked at her watch. It was six o'clock. Back in West Kensington a rich smell of dinner would be floating through the flat; the cook, watching the boiling cabbage, would be singing A Few More Years Shall Roll; her mother would be sighing; and her little brother Percy would be employed upon

25

some juvenile deviltry, the exact nature of which it was not possible to conjecture, though one could be certain that it would be something involving a deafening noise.

Claire smiled a happy smile.

4

THE offices of Messrs Nichols, Nichols, Nichols, and Nichols were in Lincoln's Inn Fields. The first Nichols had been dead since the reign of King William the Fourth, the second since the jubilee year of Queen Victoria. The remaining brace were Lord Dawlish's friend Jerry and his father, a formidable old man who knew all the shady secrets of all the noble families in England.

Bill walked up the stairs and was shown into the room where Jerry, when his father's eye was upon him, gave his daily imitation of a young man labouring with diligence and enthusiasm at the law. His father being at the moment out at lunch, the junior partner was practising putts with an umbrella and a ball of paper.

Jerry Nichols was not the typical lawyer. At Cambridge, where Bill had first made his acquaintance, he had been notable for an exuberance of which Lincoln's Inn Fields had not yet cured him. There was an airy disregard for legal formalities about him which exasperated his father, an attorney of the old school. He came to the point, directly Bill entered the room, with a speed and levity that would have appalled Nichols Senior, and must have caused the other two Nicholses to revolve in their graves.

'Halloa, Bill, old man,' he said, prodding him amiably in the waistcoat with the ferrule of the umbrella. 'How's the boy? Fine! So'm I. So you got my message? Wonderful invention, the telephone.'

'I've just come from the club.'

'Take a chair.'

'What's the matter?'

Jerry Nichols thrust Bill into a chair and seated himself on the table.

'Now look here, Bill,' he said, 'this isn't the way we usually do this sort of thing, and if the governor were here he would spend an hour and a half rambling on about testators and beneficiary legatees, and parties of the first part, and all that sort of rot. But as he isn't here I want to know, as one pal to another, what you've been doing to an old buster of the name of Nutcombe.'

'Nutcombe?'

'Nutcombe.'

'Not Ira Nutcombe?'

'Ira J. Nutcombe, formerly of Chicago, later of London, now a disembodied spirit.'

'Is he dead?'

'Yes. And he's left you something like a million pounds.'

Lord Dawlish looked at his watch.

'Joking apart, Jerry, old man,' he said, 'what did you ask me to come here for? The committee expects me to spend some of my time at the club, and if I hang about here all the afternoon I shall lose my job. Besides, I've got to get back to ask them for –'

Jerry Nichols clutched his forehead with both hands, raised both hands to heaven, and then, as if despairing of calming himself by these means, picked up a paper-weight from the desk and hurled it at a portrait of the founder of the firm, which hung over the mantelpiece. He got down from the table and crossed the room to inspect the ruins.

Then, having taken a pair of scissors and cut the cord, he allowed the portrait to fall to the floor.

He rang the bell. The prematurely-aged office-boy, who was undoubtedly destined to become a member of the firm some day, answered the ring.

'Perkins.'

'Yes, sir?'

'Inspect yonder *soufflé*.'

'Yes, sir.'

'You have observed it?'

'Yes, sir.'

'You are wondering how it got there?'

'Yes, sir.'

'I will tell you. You and I were in here, discussing certain legal minutiæ in the interests of the firm, when it suddenly fell. We both saw it and were very much surprised and startled. I soothed your nervous system by giving you this half-crown. The whole incident was very painful. Can you remember all this to tell my father when he comes in? I shall be out lunching then.'

'Yes, sir.'

'An admirable lad that,' said Jerry Nichols as the door closed. 'He has been here two years, and I have never heard him say anything except "Yes, sir." He will go far. Well, now that I am calmer let us return to your little matter. Honestly, Bill, you make me sick. When I contemplate you the iron enters my soul. You stand there talking about your tuppenny-ha'penny job as if it mattered a cent whether you kept it or not. Can't you understand plain English? Can't you realize that you can buy Brown's and turn it into a moving-picture house if you like? You're a millionaire!'

Bill's face expressed no emotion whatsoever. Outwardly he appeared unmoved. Inwardly he was a riot of bewilderment, incapable of speech. He stared at Jerry dumbly.

'We've got the will in the old oak chest,' went on Jerry Nichols. 'I won't show it to you, partly because the governor has got the key and he would have a fit if he knew that I was giving you early information like this, and partly because you wouldn't understand it. It is full of "whereases" and "perad-ventures" and "heretofores" and similar swank, and there aren't any stops in it. It takes the legal mind, like mine, to tackle wills. What it says, when you've peeled off a few of the long words which they put in to make it more interesting, is that old Nutcombe leaves you the money because you are the only man who ever did him a disinterested kindness – and what I want to get out of you is, what was the disinterested kindness? Because I'm going straight out to do it to every elderly, rich-looking man I can find till I pick a winner.'

Lord Dawlish found speech.

'Jerry, is this really true?'

'Gospel.'

'You aren't pulling my leg?'

'Pulling your leg? Of course I'm not pulling your leg. What do you take me for? I'm a dry, hard-headed lawyer. The firm of Nichols, Nichols, Nichols, and Nichols doesn't go about pulling people's legs!'

'Good Lord!'

'It appears from the will that you worked this disinterested gag, whatever it was, at Marvis Bay no longer ago than last year. Wherein you showed a lot of sense, for Ira J., having altered his will in your favour, apparently had no time before he died to alter it again in somebody else's, which he would most certainly have done if he had lived long enough, for his chief recreation seems to have been making his will. To my certain knowledge he has made three in the last two years. I've seen them. He was one of those confirmed will-makers. He got the habit at an early age, and was never able to shake it off. Do you remember anything about the man?'

'It isn't possible!'

'Anything's possible with a man cracked enough to make freak wills and not cracked enough to have them disputed on the ground of insanity. What did you do to him at Marvis Bay? Save him from drowning?'

'I cured him of slicing.'

'You did what?'

'He used to slice his approach shots. I cured him.'

'The thing begins to hang together. A certain plausibility creeps into it. The late Nutcombe was crazy about golf. The governor used to play with him now and then at Walton Heath. It was the only thing Nutcombe seemed to live for. That being so, if you got rid of his slice for him it seems to me that you earned your money. The only point that occurs to me is, how does it affect your amateur status? It looks to me as if you were now a pro.'

'But, Jerry, it's absurd. All I did was to give him a tip or two. We were the only men down there, as it was out of the season, and that drew us together. And when I spotted this slice of his I just gave him a bit of advice. I give you my word that was all. He can't have left me a fortune on the strength of that!'

'You don't tell the story right, Bill. I can guess what really happened – to wit, that you gave up all your time to helping the old fellow improve his game, regardless of the fact that it completely ruined your holiday.'

'Oh, no!'

'It's no use sitting there saying "Oh, no!" I can see you at it. The fact is, you're such an infernally good chap that something of this sort was bound to happen to you sooner or later. I think making you his heir was the only sensible thing old Nutcombe ever did. In his place I'd have done the same.'

'But he didn't even seem decently grateful at the time.'

'Probably not. He was a queer old bird. He had a most almighty row with the governor in this office only a month or two ago about absolutely nothing. They disagreed about something trivial, and old Nutcombe stalked out and never came in again. That's the sort of old bird he was.'

'Was he sane, do you think?'

'Absolutely, for legal purposes. We have three opinions from leading doctors – collected by him in case of accidents, I suppose – each of which declares him perfectly sound from the collar upward. But a man can be pretty far gone, you know, without being legally insane, and old Nutcombe – well, suppose we call him whimsical. He seems to have zigzagged between the normal and the eccentric.

'His only surviving relatives appear to be a nephew and a niece. The nephew dropped out of the running two years ago when his aunt, old Nutcombe's wife, who had divorced old Nutcombe, left him her money. This seems to have soured the old boy on the nephew, for in the first of his wills that I've seen – you remember I told you I had seen three – he leaves the niece the pile and the nephew only gets twenty pounds. Well, so far there's nothing very eccentric about old Nutcombe's proceedings. But wait!

'Six months after he had made that will he came in here and

made another. This left twenty pounds to the nephew as before, but nothing at all to the niece. Why, I don't know. There was nothing in the will about her having done anything to offend him during those six months, none of those nasty slams you see in wills about "I bequeath to my only son John one shilling and sixpence. Now perhaps he's sorry he married the cook." As far as I can make out he changed his will just as he did when he left the money to you, purely through some passing whim. Anyway, he did change it. He left the pile to support the movement those people are running for getting the Jews back to Palestine.

'He didn't seem, on second thoughts, to feel that this was quite such a brainy scheme as he had at first, and it wasn't long before he came trotting back to tear up this second will and switch back to the first one – the one leaving the money to the niece. That restoration to sanity lasted till about a month ago, when he broke loose once more and paid his final visit here to will you the contents of his stocking. This morning I see he's dead after a short illness, so you collect. Congratulations!'

Lord Dawlish had listened to this speech in perfect silence. He now rose and began to pace the room. He looked warm and uncomfortable. His demeanour, in fact, was by no means the accepted demeanour of the lucky heir.

'This is awful!' he said. 'Good Lord, Jerry, it's frightful!'

'Awful!–being left a million pounds?'

'Yes, like this. I feel like a bally thief.'

'Why on earth?'

'If it hadn't been for me this girl – what's her name?'

'Her name is Boyd – Elizabeth Boyd.'

'She would have had the whole million if it hadn't been for me. Have you told her yet?'

'She's in America. I was writing her a letter just before you came in – informal, you know, to put her out of her misery. If I had waited for the governor to let her know in the usual course of red tape we should never have got anywhere. Also one to the nephew, telling him about his twenty pounds. I believe in humane treatment on these occasions. The governor would write them a legal letter with so many "hereinbefores" in it

31

that they would get the idea that they had been left the whole pile. I just send a cheery line saying "It's no good, old top. Abandon hope," and they know just where they are. Simple and considerate.'

A glance at Bill's face moved him to further speech.

'I don't see why you should worry, Bill. How, by any stretch of the imagination, can you make out that you are to blame for this Boyd girl's misfortune? It looks to me as if these eccentric wills of old Nutcombe's came in cycles, as it were. Just as he was due for another outbreak he happened to meet you. It's a moral certainty that if he hadn't met you he would have left all his money to a Home for Superannuated Caddies or a Fund for Supplying the Deserving Poor with Niblicks. Why should you blame yourself?'

'I don't blame myself. It isn't exactly that. But – but, well, what would you feel like in my place?'

'A two-year-old.'

'Wouldn't you do anything?'

'I certainly would. By my halidom, I would! I would spend that money with a vim and speed that would make your respected ancestor, the Beau, look like a village miser.'

'You wouldn't – er – pop over to America and see whether something couldn't be arranged?'

'What!'

'I mean – suppose you were popping in any case. Suppose you had happened to buy a ticket for New York on to-morrow's boat, wouldn't you try to get in touch with this girl when you got to America, and see if you couldn't – er – fix up something?'

Jerry Nichols looked at him in honest consternation. He had always known that old Bill was a dear old ass, but he had never dreamed that he was such an infernal old ass as this.

'You aren't thinking of doing that?' he gasped.

'Well, you see, it's a funny coincidence, but I was going to America, anyhow, to-morrow. I don't see why I shouldn't try to fix up something with this girl.'

'What do you mean – fix up something? You don't suggest that you should give the money up, do you?'

'I don't know. Not exactly that, perhaps. How would it be

if I gave her half, what? Anyway, I should like to find out about her, see if she's hard up, and so on. I should like to nose round, you know, and – er – and so forth, don't you know. Where did you say the girl lived?'

'I didn't say, and I'm not sure that I shall. Honestly, Bill, you mustn't be so quixotic.'

'There's no harm in my nosing round, is there? Be a good chap and give me the address.'

'Well' – with misgivings – 'Brookport, Long Island.'

'Thanks.'

'Bill, are you really going to make a fool of yourself?'

'Not a bit of it, old chap. I'm just going to – er – '

'To nose round?'

'To nose round,' said Bill.

Jerry Nichols accompanied his friend to the door, and once more peace reigned in the offices of Nichols, Nichols, Nichols, and Nichols.

The time of a man who has at a moment's notice decided to leave his native land for a sojourn on foreign soil is necessarily taken up with a variety of occupations; and it was not till the following afternoon, on the boat at Liverpool, that Bill had leisure to write to Claire, giving her the news of what had befallen him. He had booked his ticket by a Liverpool boat in preference to one that sailed from Southampton because he had not been sure how Claire would take the news of his sudden decision to leave for America. There was the chance that she might ridicule or condemn the scheme, and he preferred to get away without seeing her. Now that he had received this astounding piece of news from Jerry Nichols he was relieved that he had acted in this way. Whatever Claire might have thought of the original scheme, there was no doubt at all what she would think of his plan of seeking out Elizabeth Boyd with a view to dividing the legacy with her.

He was guarded in his letter. He mentioned no definite figures. He wrote that Ira Nutcombe of whom they had spoken so often had most surprisingly left him in his will a large sum of money, and eased his conscience by telling himself that half of a million pounds undeniably was a large sum of money.

The addressing of the letter called for thought. She would have left Southampton with the rest of the company before it could arrive. Where was it that she said they were going next week? Portsmouth, that was it. He addressed the letter Care of The Girl and the Artist Company, to the King's Theatre, Portsmouth.

5

THE village of Brookport, Long Island, is a summer place. It lives, like the mosquitoes that infest it, entirely on its summer visitors. At the time of the death of Mr Ira Nutcombe, the only all-the-year-round inhabitants were the butcher, the grocer, the chemist, the other customary fauna of villages, and Miss Elizabeth Boyd, who rented the ramshackle farm known locally as Flack's and eked out a precarious livelihood by keeping bees.

If you take down your *Encyclopaedia Britannica,* Volume III, Aus to Bis, you will find that bees are a 'large and natural family of the zoological order *Hymenoptera,* characterized by the plumose form of many of their hairs, by the large size of the basal segment of the foot ... and by the development of a "tongue" for sucking liquid food,' the last of which peculiarities, it is interesting to note, they shared with Claude Nutcombe Boyd, Elizabeth's brother, who for quite a long time – till his money ran out – had made liquid food almost his sole means of sustenance. These things, however, are by the way. We are not such snobs as to think better or worse of a bee because it can claim kinship with the *Hymenoptera* family, nor so ill-bred as to chaff it for having large feet. The really interesting passage in the article occurs later, where it says: 'The bee industry prospers greatly in America.'

This is one of those broad statements that invite challenge. Elizabeth Boyd would have challenged it. She had not prospered greatly. With considerable trouble she contrived to pay her way, and that was all.

Again referring to the 'Encyclopaedia,' we find the words: 'Before undertaking the management of a modern apiary, the

34

beekeeper should possess a certain amount of aptitude for the pursuit.' This was possibly the trouble with Elizabeth's venture, considered from a commercial point of view. She loved bees, but she was not an expert on them. She had started her apiary with a small capital, a book of practical hints, and a second-hand queen, principally because she was in need of some occupation that would enable her to live in the country. It was the unfortunate condition of Claude Nutcombe which made life in the country a necessity. At that time he was spending the remains of the money left him by his aunt, and Elizabeth had hardly settled down at Brookport and got her venture under way when she found herself obliged to provide for Nutty a combination of home and sanatorium. It had been the poor lad's mistaken view that he could drink up all the alcoholic liquor in America.

It is a curious law of Nature that the most undeserving brothers always have the best sisters. Thrifty, plodding young men, who get up early, and do it now, and catch the employer's eye, and save half their salaries, have sisters who never speak civilly to them except when they want to borrow money. To the Claude Nutcombes of the world are vouchsafed the Elizabeths.

The great aim of Elizabeth's life was to make a new man of Nutty. It was her hope that the quiet life and soothing air of Brookport, with – unless you counted the money-in-the-slot musical box at the store – its absence of the fiercer excitements, might in time pull him together and unscramble his disordered nervous system. She liked to listen of a morning to the sound of Nutty busy in the next room with a broom and a dustpan, for in the simple lexicon of Flack's there was no such word as 'help'. The privy purse would not run to a maid. Elizabeth did the cooking and Claude Nutcombe the housework.

Several days after Claire Fenwick and Lord Dawlish, by different routes, had sailed from England, Elizabeth Boyd sat up in bed and shook her mane of hair from her eyes, yawning. Outside her window the birds were singing, and a shaft of sunlight intruded itself beneath the blind. But what definitely convinced her that it was time to get up was the plaintive note of

James, the cat, patrolling the roof of the porch. An animal of regular habits, James always called for breakfast at eight-thirty sharp.

Elizabeth got out of bed, wrapped her small body in a pink kimono, thrust her small feet into a pair of blue slippers, yawned again, and went downstairs. Having taken last night's milk from the ice-box, she went to the back door, and, having filled James's saucer, stood on the grass beside it, sniffing the morning air.

Elizabeth Boyd was twenty-one, but standing there with her hair tumbling about her shoulders she might have been taken by a not-too-close observer for a child. It was only when you saw her eyes and the resolute tilt of the chin that you realized that she was a young woman very well able to take care of herself in a difficult world. Her hair was very fair, her eyes brown and very bright, and the contrast was extraordinarily piquant. They were valiant eyes, full of spirit; eyes, also, that saw the humour of things. And her mouth was the mouth of one who laughs easily. Her chin, small like the rest of her, was strong; and in the way she held herself there was a boyish jauntiness. She looked – and was – a capable little person.

She stood besides James like a sentinel, watching over him as he breakfasted. There was a puppy belonging to one of the neighbours who sometimes lumbered over and stole James's milk, disposing of it in greedy gulps while its rightful proprietor looked on with piteous helplessness. Elizabeth was fond of the puppy, but her sense of justice was keen and she was there to check this brigandage.

It was a perfect day, cloudless and still. There was peace in the air. James, having finished his milk, began to wash himself. A squirrel climbed cautiously down from a linden tree. From the orchard came the murmur of many bees.

Aesthetically Elizabeth was fond of still, cloudless days, but experience had taught her to suspect them. As was the custom in that locality, the water supply depended on a rickety wind-wheel. It was with a dark foreboding that she returned to the kitchen and turned on one of the taps. For perhaps three seconds a stream of the dimension of a darning-needle emerged, then with a sad gurgle the tap relapsed into a stolid inaction. There is no stolidity so utter as that of a waterless tap.

'Confound it!' said Elizabeth.

She passed through the dining-room to the foot of the stairs.

'Nutty!'

There was no reply.

'Nutty, my precious lamb!'

Upstairs in the room next to her own a long, spare form began to uncurl itself in bed; a face with a receding chin and a small forehead raised itself reluctantly from the pillow, and Claude Nutcombe Boyd signalized the fact that he was awake by scowling at the morning sun and uttering an aggrieved groan.

Alas, poor Nutty! This was he whom but yesterday Broadway had known as the Speed Kid, on whom head-waiters had smiled and lesser waiters fawned; whose snake-like form had nestled in so many a front-row orchestra stall.

Where were his lobster Newburgs now, his cold quarts that were wont to set the table in a roar?

Nutty Boyd conformed as nearly as a human being may to Euclid's definition of a straight line. He was length without breadth. From boyhood's early day he had sprouted like a weed, till now in the middle twenties he gave startled strangers the conviction that it only required a sharp gust of wind to snap him in half. Lying in bed, he looked more like a length of hose-pipe than anything else. While he was unwinding himself the door opened and Elizabeth came into the room.

'Good morning, Nutty!'

'What's the time?' asked her brother, hollowly.

'Getting on towards nine. It's a lovely day. The birds are singing, the bees are buzzing, summer's in the air. It's one of those beautiful, shiny, heavenly, gorgeous days.'

A look of suspicion came into Nutty's eyes. Elizabeth was not often as lyrical as this.

'There's a catch somewhere,' he said.

'Well, as a matter of fact,' said Elizabeth, carelessly, 'the water's off again.'

'Confound it!'

37

'I said that. I'm afraid we aren't a very original family.

'What a ghastly place this is! Why can't you see old Flack and make him mend that infernal wheel?'

'I'm going to pounce on him and have another try directly I see him. Meanwhile, darling Nutty, will you get some clothes on and go round to the Smiths and ask them to lend us a pailful?'

'Oh, gosh, it's over a mile!'

'No, no, not more than three-quarters.'

'Lugging a pail that weighs a ton! The last time I went there their dog bit me.'

'I expect that was because you slunk in all doubled up, and he got suspicious. You should hold your head up and throw your chest out and stride up as if you were a military friend of the family.'

Self-pity lent Nutty eloquence.

'For Heaven's sake! You drag me out of bed at some awful hour of the morning when a rational person would just be turning in; you send me across country to fetch pailfuls of water when I'm feeling like a corpse; and on top of that you expect me to behave like a drum-major!'

'Dearest, you can wriggle on your tummy, if you like, so long as you get the fluid. We must have water. I can't fetch it. I'm a delicately-nurtured female.'

'We ought to have a man to do these ghastly jobs.'

'But we can't afford one. Just at present all I ask is to be able to pay expenses. And, as a matter of fact, you ought to be very thankful that you have got –'

'A roof over my head? I know. You needn't keep rubbing it in.'

Elizabeth flushed.

'I wasn't going to say that at all. What a pig you are sometimes, Nutty. As if I wasn't only too glad to have you here. What I was going to say was that you ought to be very thankful that you have got to draw water and hew wood –'

A look of absolute alarm came into Nutty's pallid face.

'You don't mean to say that you want some wood chopped?'

'I was speaking figuratively. I meant hustle about and work

38

in the open air. The sort of life you are leading now is what millionaires pay hundreds of dollars for at these physical-culture places. It has been the making of you.'

'I don't feel made.'

'Your nerves are ever so much better.'

'They aren't.'

Elizabeth looked at him in alarm.

'Oh, Nutty, you haven't been – seeing anything again, have you?'

'Not seeing, dreaming. I've been dreaming about monkeys. Why should I dream about monkeys if my nerves were all right?'

'I often dream about all sorts of queer things.'

'Have you ever dreamed that you were being chased up Broadway by a chimpanzee in evening dress?'

'Never mind, dear, you'll be quite all right again when you have been living this life down here a little longer.'

Nutty glared balefully at the ceiling.

'What's that darned thing up there on the ceiling? It looks like a hornet. How on earth do these things get into the house?'

'We ought to have nettings. I am going to pounce on Mr Flack about that too.'

'Thank goodness this isn't going to last much longer. It's nearly two weeks since Uncle Ira died. We ought to be hearing from the lawyers any day now. There might be a letter this morning.'

'Do you think he has left us his money?'

'Do I? Why, what else could he do with it? We are his only surviving relatives, aren't we? I've had to go through life with a ghastly name like Nutcombe as a compliment to him, haven't I? I wrote to him regularly at Christmas and on his birthday, didn't I? Well, then! I have a feeling there will be a letter from the lawyers to-day. I wish you would get dressed and go down to the post-office while I'm fetching that infernal water. I can't think why the fools haven't cabled. You would have supposed they would have thought of that.'

Elizabeth returned to her room to dress. She was conscious of a feeling that nothing was quite perfect in this world. It would be nice to have a great deal of money, for she had a scheme in her mind which called for a large capital; but she was sorry that it could come to her only through the death of her uncle, of whom, despite his somewhat forbidding personality, she had always been fond. She was also sorry that a large sum of money was coming to Nutty at that particular point in his career, just when there seemed the hope that the simple life might pull him together. She knew Nutty too well not to be able to forecast his probable behaviour under the influence of a sudden restoration of wealth.

While these thoughts were passing through her mind she happened to glance out of the window. Nutty was shambling through the garden with his pail, a bowed, shuffling pillar of gloom. As Elizabeth watched, he dropped the pail and lashed the air violently for a while. From her knowledge of bees ('It is needful to remember that bees resent outside interference and will resolutely defend themselves,' *Encyc. Brit.*, Vol. III, AUS to BIS) Elizabeth deduced that one of her little pets was annoying him. This episode concluded, Nutty resumed his pail and the journey, and at this moment there appeared over the hedge the face of Mr John Prescott, a neighbour. Mr Prescott, who had dismounted from a bicycle, called to Nutty and waved something in the air. To a stranger the performance would have been obscure, but Elizabeth understood it. Mr Prescott was intimating that he had been down to the post-office for his own letters and, as was his neighbourly custom on these occasions, had brought back also letters for Flack's.

Nutty foregathered with Mr Prescott and took the letters from him. Mr Prescott disappeared. Nutty selected one of the letters and opened it. Then, having stood perfectly still for some moments, he suddenly turned and began to run towards the house.

The mere fact that her brother, whose usual mode of progression was a languid saunter, should be actually running, was enough to tell Elizabeth that the letter which Nutty had read was from the London lawyers. No other communication could have galvanized him into such energy. Whether the contents of the letter were good or bad it was impossible at that distance to say. But when she reached the open air, just as Nutty charged up, she saw by his face that it was anguish not joy that had spurred him on. He was gasping and he bubbled unintelligible words. His little eyes gleamed wildly.

'Nutty, darling, what is it?' cried Elizabeth, every maternal instinct in her aroused.

He was thrusting a sheet of paper at her, a sheet of paper that bore the superscription of Nichols, Nichols, Nichols, and Nichols, with a London address.

'Uncle Ira –' Nutty choked. 'Twenty pounds! He's left me twenty pounds, and all the rest to a – to a man named Dawlish!'

In silence Elizabeth took the letter. It was even as he had said. A few moments before Elizabeth had been regretting the imminent descent of wealth upon her brother. Now she was inconsistent enough to boil with rage at the shattering blow which had befallen him. That she, too, had lost her inheritance hardly occurred to her. Her thoughts were all for Nutty. It did not need the sight of him, gasping and gurgling before her, to tell her how overwhelming was his disappointment.

It was useless to be angry with the deceased Mr Nutcombe. He was too shadowy a mark. Besides, he was dead. The whole current of her wrath turned upon the supplanter, this Lord Dawlish. She pictured him as a crafty adventurer, a wretched fortune-hunter. For some reason or other she imagined him a sinister person with a black moustache, a face thin and hawk-like, and unpleasant eyes. That was the sort of man who would be likely to fasten his talons into poor Uncle Ira.

She had never hated any one in her life before, but as she stood there at that moment she felt that she loathed and detested William Lord Dawlish – unhappy, well-meaning Bill, who only a few hours back had set foot on American soil in his desire to nose round and see if something couldn't be arranged.

Nutty fetched the water. Life is like that. There is nothing clean-cut about it, no sense of form. Instead of being permitted to concentrate his attention on his tragedy Nutty had to trudge three-quarters of a mile, conciliate a bull-terrier, and trudge back again carrying a heavy pail. It was as if one of the heroes of Greek drama, in the middle of his big scene, had been asked to run round the corner to a provision store.

The exercise did not act as a restorative. The blow had been too sudden, too overwhelming. Nutty's reason – such as it was – tottered on its throne. Who was Lord Dawlish? What had he done to ingratiate himself with Uncle Ira? By what insidious means, with what devilish cunning, had he wormed his way into the old man's favour? These were the questions that vexed Nutty's mind when he was able to think at all coherently.

Back at the farm Elizabeth cooked breakfast and awaited her brother's return with a sinking heart. She was a soft-hearted girl, easily distressed by the sight of suffering; and she was aware that Nutty was scarcely of the type that masks its woes behind a brave and cheerful smile. Her heart bled for Nutty.

There was a weary step outside. Nutty entered, slopping water. One glance at his face was enough to tell Elizabeth that she had formed a too conservative estimate of his probable gloom. Without a word he coiled his long form in a chair. There was silence in the stricken house.

'What's the time?'

Elizabeth glanced at her watch.

'Half-past nine.'

'About now,' said Nutty, sepulchrally, 'the blighter is ringing for his man to prepare his bally bath and lay out his gold-leaf underwear. After that he will drive down to the bank and draw some of our money.'

The day passed wearily for Elizabeth. Nutty having the air of one who is still engaged in picking up the pieces, she had not the heart to ask him to play his customary part in the household duties, so she washed the dishes and made the beds herself. After that she attended to the bees. After that she cooked lunch.

Nutty was not chatty at lunch. Having observed 'About now the blighter is cursing the waiter for bringing the wrong brand of champagne,' he relapsed into a silence which he did not again break.

Elizabeth was busy again in the afternoon. At four o'clock,

feeling tired out, she went to her room to lie down until the next of her cycle of domestic duties should come round.

It was late when she came downstairs, for she had fallen asleep. The sun had gone down. Bees were winging their way heavily back to the hives with their honey. She went out into the grounds to try to find Nutty. There had been no signs of him in the house. There were no signs of him about the grounds. It was not like him to have taken a walk, but it seemed the only possibility. She went back to the house to wait. Eight o'clock came, and nine, and it was then the truth dawned upon her – Nutty had escaped. He had slipped away and gone up to New York.

6

LORD DAWLISH sat in the New York flat which had been lent him by his friend Gates. The hour was half-past ten in the evening; the day, the second day after the exodus of Nutty Boyd from the farm. Before him on the table lay a letter. He was smoking pensively.

Lord Dawlish had found New York enjoyable, but a trifle fatiguing. There was much to be seen in the city, and he had made the mistake of trying to see it all at once. It had been his intention, when he came home after dinner that night, to try to restore the balance of things by going to bed early. He had sat up longer than he had intended, because he had been thinking about this letter.

Immediately upon his arrival in America, Bill had sought out a lawyer and instructed him to write to Elizabeth Boyd, offering her one-half of the late Ira Nutcombe's money. He had had time during the voyage to think the whole matter over, and this seemed to him the only possible course. He could not keep it all. He would feel like the despoiler of the widow and the orphan. Nor would it be fair to Claire to give it all up. If he halved the legacy everybody would be satisfied.

That at least had been his view until Elizabeth's reply had arrived. It was this reply that lay on the table – a brief, formal note, setting forth Miss Boyd's absolute refusal to accept any portion of the money. This was a development which Bill had not foreseen, and he was feeling baffled. What was the next step? He had smoked many pipes in the endeavour to find an answer to this problem, and was lighting another when the door-bell rang.

He opened the door and found himself confronting an extraordinarily tall and thin young man in evening-dress.

Lord Dawlish was a little startled. He had taken it for granted, when the bell rang, that his visitor was Tom, the liftman from downstairs, a friendly soul who hailed from London and had been dropping in at intervals during the past two days to acquire the latest news from his native land. He stared at this changeling inquiringly. The solution of the mystery came with the stranger's first words –

'Is Gates in ?'

He spoke eagerly, as if Gates were extremely necessary to his well-being. It distressed Lord Dawlish to disappoint him, but there was nothing else to be done.

'Gates is in London,' he said.

'What! When did he go there?'

'About four months ago.'

'May I come in a minute?'

'Yes, rather, do.'

He led the way into the sitting-room. The stranger gave abruptly in the middle, as if he were being folded up by some invisible agency, and in this attitude sank into a chair, where he lay back looking at Bill over his knees, like a sorrowful sheep peering over a sharp-pointed fence.

'You're from England, aren't you?'

'Yes.'

'Been in New York long?'

'Only a couple of days.'

The stranger folded himself up another foot or so until his knees were higher than his head, and lit a cigarette.

'The curse of New York,' he said, mournfully, 'is the way everything changes in it. You can't take your eyes off it for a minute. The population's always shifting. It's like a railway

44

station. You go away for a bit and come back and try to find your old pals, and they're all gone: Ike's in Arizona, Mike's in a sanatorium, Spike's in jail, and nobody seems to know where the rest of them have got to. I came up from the country two days ago, expecting to find the old gang along Broadway the same as ever, and I'm dashed if I've been able to put my hands on one of them! Not a single, solitary one of them! And it's only six months since I was here last.'

Lord Dawlish made sympathetic noises.

'Of course,' proceeded the other, 'the time of year may have something to do with it. Living down in the country you lose count of time, and I forgot that it was July, when people go out of the city. I guess that must be what happened. I used to know all sorts of fellows, actors and fellows like that, and they're all away somewhere. I tell you,' he said, with pathos, 'I never knew I could be so infernally lonesome as I have been these last two days. If I had known what a rotten time I was going to have I would never have left Brookport.'

'Brookport!'

'It's a place down on Long Island.'

Bill was not by nature a plotter, but the mere fact of travelling under an assumed name had developed a streak of wariness in him. He checked himself just as he was about to ask his companion if he happened to know a Miss Elizabeth Boyd, who also lived at Brookport. It occurred to him that the question would invite a counter-question as to his own knowledge of Miss Boyd, and he knew that he would not be able to invent a satisfactory answer to that offhand.

'This evening,' said the thin young man, resuming his dirge, 'I was sweating my brain to try to think of somebody I could hunt up in this ghastly, deserted city. It isn't so easy, you know, to think of fellows' names and addresses. I can get the names all right, but unless the fellow's in the telephone-book, I'm done. Well, I was trying to think of some of my pals who might still be around the place, and I remembered Gates. Remembered his address, too, by a miracle. You're a pal of his, of course?'

'Yes, I knew him in London.'

'Oh, I see. And when you came over here he lent you his flat? By the way, I didn't get your name?'

'My name's Chalmers.'

'Well, as I say, I remembered Gates and came down here to look him up. We used to have a lot of good times together a year ago. And now he's gone too!'

'Did you want to see him about anything important?'

'Well, it's important to me. I wanted him to come out to supper. You see, it's this way: I'm giving supper to-night to a girl who's in that show at the Forty-ninth Street Theatre, a Miss Leonard, and she insists on bringing a pal. She says the pal is a good sport, which sounds all right –' Bill admitted that it sounded all right. 'But it makes the party three And of all the infernal things a party of three is the ghastliest.'

Having delivered himself of this undeniable truth the stranger slid a little farther into his chair and paused. 'Look here, what are you doing to-night?' he said.

'I was thinking of going to bed.'

'Going to bed!' The stranger's voice was shocked, as if he had heard blasphemy. 'Going to bed at half-past ten in New York! My dear chap, what you want is a bit of supper. Why don't you come along?'

Amiability was, perhaps, the leading quality of Lord Dawlish's character. He did not want to have to dress and go out to supper, but there was something almost pleading in the eyes that looked at him between the sharply-pointed knees.

'It's awfully good of you –' He hesitated.

'Not a bit; I wish you would. You would be a life-saver.'

Bill felt that he was in for it. He got up.

'You will?' said the other. 'Good boy! You go and get into some clothes and come along. I'm sorry, what did you say your name was?'

'Chalmers.'

'Mine's Boyd – Nutcombe Boyd.'

'Boyd!' cried Bill.

Nutty took his astonishment, which was too great to be concealed, as a compliment. He chuckled.

'I thought you would know the name if you were a pal of

46

Gates's. I expect he's always talking about me. You see, I was pretty well known in this old place before I had to leave it.'

Bill walked down the long passage to his bedroom with no trace of the sleepiness which had been weighing on him five minutes before. He was galvanized by a superstitious thrill. It was fate, Elizabeth Boyd's brother turning up like this and making friendly overtures right on top of that letter from her. This astonishing thing could not have been better arranged if he had planned it himself. From what little he had seen of Nutty he gathered that the latter was not hard to make friends with. It would be a simple task to cultivate his acquaintance. And having done so, he could renew negotiations with Elizabeth. The desire to rid himself of half the legacy had become a fixed idea with Bill. He had the impression that he could not really feel clean again until he had made matters square with his conscience in this respect. He felt that he was probably a fool to take that view of the thing, but that was the way he was built and there was no getting away from it.

This irruption of Nutty Boyd into his life was an omen. It meant that all was not yet over. He was conscious of a mild surprise that he had ever intended to go to bed. He felt now as if he never wanted to go to bed again. He felt exhilarated.

In these days one cannot say that a supper-party is actually given in any one place. Supping in New York has become a peripatetic pastime. The supper-party arranged by Nutty Boyd was scheduled to start at Reigelheimer's on Forty-second Street, and it was there that the revellers assembled.

Nutty and Bill had been there a few minutes when Miss Daisy Leonard arrived with her friend. And from that moment Bill was never himself again.

The Good Sport was, so to speak, an outsize in Good Sports. She loomed up behind the small and demure Miss Leonard like a liner towed by a tug. She was big, blonde, skittish, and exuberant; she wore a dress like the sunset of a fine summer evening, and she effervesced with spacious good will to all men. She was one of those girls who splash into public places like stones into quiet pools. Her form was large, her eyes were large, her teeth were large, and her voice was large. She overwhelmed Bill. She hit his astounded consciousness like a shell. She gave him a buzzing in the ears. She was not so much a Good Sport as some kind of an explosion.

He was still reeling from the spiritual impact with this female tidal wave when he became aware, as one who, coming out of a swoon, hears voices faintly, that he was being addressed by Miss Leonard. To turn from Miss Leonard's friend to Miss Leonard herself was like hearing the falling of gentle rain after a thunderstorm. For a moment he revelled in the sense of being soothed; then, as he realized what she was saying, he started violently. Miss Leonard was looking at him curiously.

'I beg your pardon?' said Bill.

'I'm sure I've met you before, Mr Chalmers.'

'Er – really?'

'But I can't think where.'

'I'm sure,' said the Good Sport, languishingly, like a sentimental siege-gun, 'that if I had ever met Mr Chalmers before I shouldn't have forgotten him.'

'You're English, aren't you?' asked Miss Leonard.

'Yes.'

The Good Sport said she was crazy about Englishmen.

'I thought so from your voice.'

The Good Sport said that she was crazy about the English accent.

'It must have been in London that I met you. I was in the revue at the Alhambra last year.'

'By George, I wish I had seen you!' interjected the infatuated Nutty.

The Good Sport said that she was crazy about London.

'I seem to remember,' went on Miss Leonard, 'meeting you out at supper. Do you know a man named Delaney in the Coldstream Guards?'

Bill would have liked to deny all knowledge of Delaney, though the latter was one of his best friends, but his natural honesty prevented him.

'I'm sure I met you at a supper he gave at Oddy's one Friday night. We all went on to Covent Garden. Don't you remember?'

'Talking of supper,' broke in Nutty, earning Bill's hearty gratitude thereby, 'where's the dashed head-waiter? I want to find my table.'

He surveyed the restaurant with a melancholy eye.

'Everything changed!' He spoke sadly, as Ulysses might have done when his boat put in at Ithaca. 'Every darned thing different since I was here last. New waiter, head-waiter I never saw before in my life, different-coloured carpet – '

'Cheer up, Nutty, old thing!' said Miss Leonard. 'You'll feel better when you've had something to eat. I hope you had the sense to tip the head-waiter, or there won't be any table. Funny how these places go up and down in New York. A year ago the whole management would turn out and kiss you if you looked like spending a couple of dollars here. Now it costs the earth to get in at all.'

'Why's that?' asked Nutty.

'Lady Pauline Wetherby, of course. Didn't you know this was where she danced?'

'Never heard of her,' said Nutty, in a sort of ecstasy of wistful gloom. 'That will show you how long I've been away. Who is she?'

Miss Leonard invoked the name of Mike.

'Don't you ever get the papers in your village, Nutty?'

'I never read the papers. I don't suppose I've read a paper for years. I can't stand 'em. Who is Lady Pauline Wetherby?'

'She does Greek dances – at least, I suppose they're Greek. They all are nowadays, unless they're Russian. She's an English peeress.'

Miss Leonard's friend said she was crazy about these picturesque old English families; and they went in to supper.

Looking back on the evening later and reviewing its leading features, Lord Dawlish came to the conclusion that he never completely recovered from the first shock of the Good Sport. He was conscious all the time of a dream-like feeling, as if he were watching himself from somewhere outside himself. From some conning-tower in this fourth dimension he perceived himself eating broiled lobster and drinking champagne and heard himself bearing an adequate part in the conversation; but his movements were largely automatic.

Time passed. It seemed to Lord Dawlish, watching from without, that things were livening up. He seemed to perceive a quickening of the *tempo* of the revels, an added abandon. Nutty was getting quite bright. He had the air of one who recalls the good old days, of one who in familiar scenes re-enacts the joys of his vanished youth. The chastened melancholy induced by many months of fetching of pails of water, of scrubbing floors with a mop, and of jumping like a firecracker to avoid excited bees had been purged from him by the lights and the music and the wine. He was telling a long anecdote, laughing at it, throwing a crust of bread at an adjacent waiter, and refilling his glass at the same time. It is not easy to do all these things simultaneously, and the fact that Nutty did them with notable success was proof that he was picking up.

Miss Daisy Leonard was still demure, but as she had just slipped a piece of ice down the back of Nutty's neck one may assume that she was feeling at her ease and had overcome any diffidence or shyness which might have interfered with her complete enjoyment of the festivities. As for the Good Sport, she was larger, blonder, and more exuberant than ever and she was addressing someone as 'Bill'.

Perhaps the most remarkable phenomenon of the evening, as it advanced, was the change it wrought in Lord Dawlish's attitude toward this same Good Sport. He was not conscious of the beginning of the change; he awoke to the realization of it suddenly. At the beginning of supper his views on her had been definite and clear. When they had first been introduced to each other he had had a stunned feeling that this sort of thing ought not to be allowed at large, and his battered brain had instinctively recalled that line of Tennyson: 'The curse is come upon me.' But now, warmed with food and drink and smoking an excellent cigar, he found that a gentler, more charitable mood had descended upon him.

He argued with himself in extenuation of the girl's peculiar idiosyncrasies. Was it, he asked himself, altogether her fault that she was so massive and spoke as if she were addressing an open-air meeting in a strong gale? Perhaps it was hereditary. Perhaps her father had been a circus giant and her mother the strong woman of the troupe. And for the unrestraint of her manner defective training in early girlhood would account. He began to regard her with a quiet, kindly commiseration, which in its turn changed into a sort of brotherly affection. He discovered that he liked her. He liked her very much. She was so big and jolly and robust, and spoke in such a clear, full voice. He was glad that she was patting his hand. He was glad that he had asked her to call him Bill.

People were dancing now. It has been claimed by patriots that American dyspeptics lead the world. This supremacy, though partly due, no doubt, to vast supplies of pie absorbed in youth, may be attributed to a certain extent also to the national habit of dancing during meals. Lord Dawlish had that sturdy reverence for his interior organism which is the birthright of every Briton. And at the beginning of supper he had resolved that nothing should induce him to court disaster in this fashion. But as the time went on he began to waver.

The situation was awkward. Nutty and Miss Leonard were repeatedly leaving the table to tread the measure, and on these occasions the Good Sport's wistfulness was a haunting reproach. Nor was the spectacle of Nutty in action without its effect on Bill's resolution. Nutty dancing was a sight to stir the most stolid.

Bill wavered. The music had started again now, one of those twentieth-century eruptions of sound that begin like a train going through a tunnel and continue like audible electric shocks, that set the feet tapping beneath the table and the spine thrilling with an unaccustomed exhilaration. Every drop of blood in his body cried to him 'Dance!' He could resist no longer.

'Shall we?' he said.

Bill should not have danced. He was an estimable young man, honest, amiable, with high ideals. He had played an excellent game of football at the university; his golf handicap was plus two; and he was no mean performer with the gloves. But we all of us have our limitations, and Bill had his. He was not a good dancer. He was energetic, but he required more elbow room than the ordinary dancing floor provides. As a dancer, in fact, he closely resembled a Newfoundland puppy trying to run across a field.

It takes a good deal to daunt the New York dancing man, but the invasion of the floor by Bill and the Good Sport undoubtedly caused a profound and even painful sensation. Linked together they formed a living projectile which might well have intimidated the bravest. Nutty was their first victim. They caught him in mid-step – one of those fancy steps which he was just beginning to exhume from the cobwebbed recesses of his memory – and swept him away. After which they descended resistlessly upon a stout gentleman of middle age, chiefly conspicuous for the glittering diamonds which he wore and the stoical manner in which he danced to and fro on one spot of not more than a few inches in size in the exact centre of the room. He had apparently staked out a claim to this small spot, a claim which the other dancers had decided to respect; but Bill and the Good Sport, coming up from behind, had him two yards away from it at the first impact. Then, scattering apologies broadcast like a medieval monarch distributing largesse, Bill whirled his partner round by sheer muscular force and began what he intended to be a movement toward the farther corner, skirting the edge of the floor. It was his simple belief that there was more safety there than in the middle.

He had not reckoned with Heinrich Joerg. Indeed, he was not aware of Heinrich Joerg's existence. Yet fate was shortly to bring them together, with far-reaching results Heinrich Joerg had left the Fatherland a good many years before with the prudent purpose of escaping military service. After various vicissitudes in the land of his adoption – which it would be extremely interesting to relate, but which must wait for a more favourable opportunity – he had secured a useful and not ill-recompensed situation as one of the staff of Reigelheimer's Restaurant. He was, in point of fact, a waiter, and he comes into the story at this point bearing a tray full of glasses, knives, forks, and pats of butter on little plates. He was setting a table for some new arrivals, and in order to obtain more scope for that task he had left the crowded aisle beyond the table and come round to the edge of the dancing-floor.

He should not have come out on to the dancing-floor. In another moment he was admitting that himself. For just as he was lowering his tray and bending over the table in the pursuance of his professional duties, along came Bill at his customary high rate of speed, propelling his partner before him, and for the first time since he left home Heinrich was conscious of a regret that he had done so. There are worse things than military service!

It was the table that saved Bill. He clutched at it and it supported him. He was thus enabled to keep the Good Sport from falling and to assist Heinrich to rise from the morass of glasses, knives, and pats of butter in which he was wallowing. Then, the dance having been abandoned by mutual consent, he helped his now somewhat hysterical partner back to their table.

Remorse came upon Bill. He was sorry that he had danced; sorry that he had upset Heinrich; sorry that he had subjected the Good Sport's nervous system to such a strain; sorry that so much glass had been broken and so many pats of butter bruised beyond repair. But of one thing, even in that moment of bleak regrets, he was distinctly glad, and that was that all these things had taken place three thousand miles away from Claire Fenwick. He had not been appearing at his best, and he was glad that Claire had not seen him.

As he sat and smoked the remains of his cigar, while renewing his apologies and explanations to his partner and soothing the ruffled Nutty with well-chosen condolences, he wondered idly what Claire was doing at that moment.

Claire at that moment, having been an astonished eye-witness of the whole performance, was resuming her seat at a table at the other end of the room.

7

THERE were two reasons why Lord Dawlish was unaware of Claire Fenwick's presence at Reigelheimer's Restaurant: Reigelheimer's is situated in a basement below a ten-storey building, and in order to prevent this edifice from falling into his patrons' soup the proprietor had been obliged to shore up his ceiling with massive pillars. One of these protruded itself between the table which Nutty had secured for his supper-party and the table at which Claire was sitting with her friend, Lady Wetherby, and her steamer acquaintance, Mr Dudley Pickering. That was why Bill had not seen Claire from where he sat; and the reason that he had not seen her when he left his seat and began to dance was that he was not one of your dancers who glance airily about them. When Bill danced he danced.

He would have been stunned with amazement if he had known that Claire was at Reigelheimer's that night And yet it would have been remarkable, seeing that she was the guest of Lady Wetherby, if she had not been there. When you have travelled three thousand miles to enjoy the hospitality of a friend who does near-Greek dances at a popular restaurant, the least you can do is to go to the restaurant and watch her step. Claire had arrived with Polly Wetherby and Mr Dudley Pickering at about the time when Nutty, his gloom melting rapidly, was instructing the waiter to open the second bottle.

Of Claire's movements between the time when she secured her ticket at the steamship offices at Southampton and the moment when she entered Reigelheimer's Restaurant it is not necessary to give a detailed record. She had had the usual experiences of the ocean voyager. She had fed, read, and gone to bed. The only notable event in her trip had been her intimacy with Mr Dudley Pickering.

Dudley Pickering was a middle-aged Middle Westerner, who by thrift and industry had amassed a considerable fortune out of automobiles. Everybody spoke well of Dudley Pickering. The papers spoke well of him, Bradstreet spoke well of him, and he spoke well of himself. On board the liner he had poured the saga of his life into Claire's attentive ears, and there was a gentle sweetness in her manner which encouraged Mr Pickering mightily, for he had fallen in love with Claire on sight.

It would seem that a schoolgirl in these advanced days would know what to do when she found that a man worth millions was in love with her; yet there were factors in the situation which gave Claire pause. Lord Dawlish, of course, was one of them. She had not mentioned Lord Dawlish to Mr Pickering, and – doubtless lest the sight of it might pain him – she had abstained from wearing her engagement ring during the voyage. But she had not completely lost sight of the fact that she was engaged to Bill. Another thing that caused her to hesitate was the fact that Dudley Pickering, however wealthy, was a most colossal bore. As far as Claire could ascertain on their short acquaintance, he had but one subject of conversation – automobiles.

To Claire an automobile was a shiny thing with padded seats, in which you rode if you were lucky enough to know somebody who owned one. She had no wish to go more deeply into the matter. Dudley Pickering's attitude towards automobiles, on the other hand, more nearly resembled that of a surgeon towards the human body. To him a car was something to dissect, something with an interior both interesting to explore and fascinating to talk about. Claire listened with a radiant display of interest, but she had her doubts as to whether any amount of money would make it worth while to undergo this sort of thing for life. She was still in this hesitant frame of mind when she entered Reigelheimer's Restaurant, and it perturbed her that she could not come to some definite decision on Mr Pickering, for those subtle signs which every woman can recognize and interpret told her that the latter, having paved the way by talking machinery for a week, was about to boil over and speak of higher things.

At the very next opportunity, she was certain, he intended to propose.

The presence of Lady Wetherby acted as a temporary check on the development of the situation, but after they had been seated at their table a short time the lights of the restaurant were suddenly lowered, a coloured limelight became manifest near the roof, and classical music made itself heard from the fiddles in the orchestra.

You could tell it was classical, because the banjo players were leaning back and chewing gum; and in New York restaurants only death or a classical speciality can stop banjoists.

There was a spatter of applause, and Lady Wetherby rose.

'This,' she explained to Claire, 'is where I do my stunt. Watch it. I invented the steps myself. Classical stuff. It's called the Dream of Psyche.'

It was difficult for one who knew her as Claire did to associate Polly Wetherby with anything classical. On the road, in England, when they had been fellow-members of the Number Two company of *The Heavenly Waltz*, Polly had been remarkable chiefly for a fund of humorous anecdote and a gift, amounting almost to genius, for doing battle with militant landladies. And renewing their intimacy after a hiatus of a little less than a year Claire had found her unchanged.

It was a truculent affair, this Dream of Psyche. It was not so much dancing as shadow boxing. It began mildly enough to the accompaniment of *pizzicato* strains from the orchestra – Psyche in her training quarters. *Rallentando* – Psyche punching the bag. *Diminuendo* – Psyche using the medicine ball. *Presto* – Psyche doing road work. *Forte* – The night of the fight. And then things began to move to a climax. With the fiddles working themselves to the bone and the piano bounding under its persecutor's blows, Lady Wetherby ducked, side-stepped, rushed, and sprang, moving her arms in a manner that may have been classical Greek, but to the untrained eye looked much more like the last round of some open-air bout.

It was half-way through the exhibition, when you could smell the sawdust and hear the seconds shouting advice under the ropes, that Claire, who, never having seen anything in her life like this extraordinary performance, had been staring spellbound, awoke to the realization that Dudley Pickering was proposing to her. It required a woman's intuition to divine this fact, for Mr Pickering was not coherent. He did not go straight

56

to the point. He rambled. But Claire understood, and it came to her that this thing had taken her before she was ready. In a brief while she would have to give an answer of some sort, and she had not clearly decided what answer she meant to give.

Then, while he was still skirting his subject, before he had wandered to what he really wished to say, the music stopped, the applause broke out again, and Lady Wetherby returned to the table like a pugilist seeking his corner at the end of a round. Her face was flushed and she was breathing hard.

'They pay me money for that!' she observed, genially. 'Can you beat it?'

The spell was broken. Mr Pickering sank back in his chair in a punctured manner. And Claire, making monosyllabic replies to her friend's remarks, was able to bend her mind to the task of finding out how she stood on this important Pickering issue. That he would return to the attack as soon as possible she knew; and the next time she must have her attitude clearly defined one way or the other.

Lady Wetherby, having got the Dance of Psyche out of her system, and replaced it with a glass of iced coffee, was inclined for conversation.

'Algie called me up on the phone this evening, Claire.'

'Yes?'

Claire was examining Mr Pickering with furtive side glances. He was not handsome, nor, on the other hand, was he repulsive. 'Undistinguished' was the adjective that would have described him. He was inclined to stoutness, but not unpardonably so; his hair was thin, but he was not aggressively bald; his face was dull, but certainly not stupid. There was nothing in his outer man which his millions would not offset. As regarded his other qualities, his conversation was certainly not exhilarating. But that also was not, under certain conditions, an unforgivable thing. No, looking at the matter all round and weighing it with care, the real obstacle, Claire decided, was not any quality or lack of qualities in Dudley Pickering – it was Lord Dawlish and the simple fact that it would be extremely difficult, if she discarded him in favour of a richer man without any ostensible cause, to retain her self-respect.

'I think he's weakening.'

'Yes?'

Yes, that was the crux of the matter. She wanted to retain her good opinion of herself. And in order to achieve that end it was essential that she find some excuse, however trivial, for breaking off the engagement.

'Yes?'

A waiter approached the table.

'Mr Pickering!'

The thwarted lover came to life with a start.

'Eh?'

'A gentleman wishes to speak to you on the telephone.'

'Oh, yes. I was expecting a long-distance call, Lady Wetherby, and left word I would be here. Will you excuse me?'

Lady Wetherby watched him as he bustled across the room.

'What do you think of him, Claire?'

'Mr Pickering? I think he's very nice.'

'He admires you frantically. I hoped he would That's why I wanted you to come over on the same ship with him.'

'Polly! I had no notion you were such a schemer.'

'I would just love to see you two fix it up,' continued Lady Wetherby, earnestly. 'He may not be what you might call a genius, but he's a darned good sort; and all his millions help, don't they? You don't want to overlook these millions, Claire!'

'I do like Mr Pickering.'

'Claire, he asked me if you were engaged.'

'What!'

'When I told him you weren't, he beamed Honestly, you've only got to lift your little finger and – Oh, good Lord, there's Algie!'

Claire looked up. A dapper, trim little man of about forty was threading his way among the tables in their direction. It was a year since Claire had seen Lord Wetherby, but she recognized him at once. He had a red, weather-beaten face with a suspicion of side-whiskers, small, pink-rimmed eyes with sandy eyebrows, the smoothest of sandy hair, and a chin so cleanly shaven that it was difficult to believe that hair had ever grown there. Although his evening-dress was perfect in every detail, he conveyed a subtle suggestion of horsiness. He reached the table and sat down without invitation in the vacant chair.

'Pauline!' he said, sorrowfully.

'Algie!' said Lady Wetherby, tensely. 'I don't know what you've come here for, and I don't remember asking you to sit down and put your elbows on that table, but I want to begin by saying that I will not be called Pauline. My name's Polly. You've got a way of saying Pauline, as if it were a gentlemanly cuss-word, that makes me want to scream. And while you're about it, why don't you say how-d'you-do to Claire? You ought to remember her, she was my bridesmaid.'

'How do you do, Miss Fenwick. Of course, I remember you perfectly. I'm glad to see you again.'

'And now, Algie, what is it? Why have you come here?' Lord Wetherby looked doubtfully at Claire. 'Oh, that's all right,' said Lady Wetherby. 'Claire knows all about it – I told her.'

'Then I appeal to Miss Fenwick, if, as you say, she knows all the facts of the case, to say whether it is reasonable to expect a man of my temperament, a nervous, highly-strung artist, to welcome the presence of snakes at the breakfast-table. I trust that I am not an unreasonable man, but I decline to admit that a long, green snake is a proper thing to keep about the house.'

'You had no right to strike the poor thing.'

'In that one respect I was perhaps a little hasty. I happened to be stirring my tea at the moment his head rose above the edge of the table. I was not entirely myself that morning. My nerves were somewhat disordered. I had lain awake much of the night planning a canvas.'

'Planning a what?'

'A canvas – a picture.'

Lady Wetherby turned to Claire.

'I want you to listen to Algie, Claire. A year ago he did not know one end of a paint-brush from the other. He didn't know he had any nerves. If you had brought him the artistic temperament on a plate with a bit of watercress round it, he wouldn't have recognized it. And now, just because he's got a studio, he thinks he has a right to go up in the air if you speak to him suddenly and run about the place hitting snakes with teaspoons as if he were Michelangelo!'

'You do me an injustice. It is true that as an artist I developed late – But why should we quarrel? If it will help to pave the way to a renewed understanding between us, I am prepared to apologize for striking Clarence. That is conciliatory, I think, Miss Fenwick?'

'Very.'

'Miss Fenwick considers my attitude conciliatory.'

'It's something,' admitted Lady Wetherby, grudgingly.

Lord Wetherby drained the whisky-and-soda which Dudley Pickering had left behind him, and seemed to draw strength from it, for he now struck a firmer note.

'But, though expressing regret for my momentary loss of self-control, I cannot recede from the position I have taken up as regards the essential unfitness of Clarence's presence in the home.'

Lady Wetherby looked despairingly at Claire.

'The very first words I heard Algie speak, Claire, were at Newmarket during the three o'clock race one May afternoon. He was hanging over the rail, yelling like an Indian, and what he was yelling was, "Come on, you blighter, come on! By the living jingo, Brickbat wins in a walk!" And now he's talking about receding from essential positions! Oh, well, he wasn't an artist then!'

'My dear Pau – Polly. I am purposely picking my words on the present occasion in order to prevent the possibility of further misunderstandings. I consider myself an ambassador.'

'You would be shocked if you knew what I consider you!'

'I am endeavouring to the best of my ability – '

'Algie, listen to me! I am quite calm at present, but there's no knowing how soon I may hit you with a chair if you don't come to earth quick and talk like an ordinary human being. What is it that you are driving at?'

'Very well, it's this: I'll come home if you get rid of that snake.'

'Never!'

'It's surely not much to ask of you, Polly?'

60

'I won't!'

Lord Wetherby sighed.

'When I led you to the altar,' he said, reproachfully, 'you promised to love, honour, and obey me. I thought at the time it was a bit of swank!'

Lady Wetherby's manner thawed. She became more friendly.

'When you talk like that, Algie, I feel there's hope for you after all. That's how you used to talk in the dear old days when you'd come to me to borrow half-a-crown to put on a horse! Listen, now that at last you seem to be getting more reasonable; I wish I could make you understand that I don't keep Clarence for sheer love of him. He's a commercial asset. He's an advertisement. You must know that I have got to have something to – '

'I admit that may be so as regards the monkey, Eustace. Monkeys as aids to publicity have, I believe, been tested and found valuable by other artistes. I am prepared to accept Eustace, but the snake is worthless.'

'Oh, you don't object to Eustace, then?'

'I do strongly, but I concede his uses.'

'You would live in the same house as Eustace?'

'I would endeavour to do so. But not in the same house as Eustace and Clarence.'

There was a pause.

'I don't know that I'm so stuck on Clarence myself,' said Lady Wetherby, weakly.

'My darling!'

'Wait a minute. I've not said I would get rid of him.'

'But you will?'

Lady Wetherby's hesitation lasted but a moment. 'All right, Algie. I'll send him to the Zoo to-morrow.'

'My precious pet!'

A hand, reaching under the table, enveloped Claire's in a loving clasp.

From the look on Lord Wetherby's face she supposed that he was under the delusion that he was bestowing this attention on his wife.

'You know, Algie, darling,' said Lady Wetherby, melting

completely, 'when you get that yearning note in your voice I just flop and take the full count.'

'My sweetheart, when I saw you doing that Dream of What's-the-girl's-bally-name dance just now, it was all I could do to keep from rushing out on to the floor and hugging you.'

'Algie!'

'Polly!'

'Do you mind letting go of my hand, please, Lord Wetherby?' said Claire, on whom these saccharine exchanges were beginning to have a cloying effect.

For a moment Lord Wetherby seemed somewhat confused, but, pulling himself together, he covered his embarrassment with a pomposity that blended poorly with his horsy appearance.

'Married life, Miss Fenwick,' he said, 'as you will no doubt discover some day, must always be a series of mutual compromises, of cheerful give and take. The lamp of love –'

His remarks were cut short by a crash at the other end of the room. There was a sharp cry and the splintering of glass. The place was full of a sudden, sharp confusion They jumped up with one accord. Lady Wetherby spilled her iced coffee; Lord Wetherby dropped the lamp of love. Claire, who was nearest the pillar that separated them from the part of the restaurant where the accident had happened, was the first to see what had taken place.

A large man, dancing with a large girl, appeared to have charged into a small waiter, upsetting him and his tray and the contents of his tray. The various actors in the drama were now engaged in sorting themselves out from the ruins. The man had his back toward her, and it seemed to Claire that there was something familiar about that back. Then he turned, and she recognized Lord Dawlish.

She stood transfixed. For a moment surprise was her only emotion. How came Bill to be in America? Then other feelings blended with her surprise. It is a fact that Lord Dawlish was looking singularly uncomfortable.

Claire's eyes travelled from Bill to his partner and took in with one swift feminine glance her large, exuberant blondeness.

There is no denying that, seen with a somewhat biased eye, the Good Sport resembled rather closely a poster advertising a revue.

Claire returned to her seat. Lord and Lady Wetherby continued to talk, but she allowed them to conduct the conversation without her assistance.

'You're very quiet, Claire,' said Polly.

'I'm thinking.'

'A very good thing, too, so they tell me. I've never tried it myself. Algie, darling, he was a bad boy to leave his nice home, wasn't he? He didn't deserve to have his hand held.'

8

IT had been a great night for Nutty Boyd. If the vision of his sister Elizabeth, at home at the farm speculating sadly on the whereabouts of her wandering boy, ever came before his mental eye he certainly did not allow it to interfere with his appreciation of the festivities. At Frolics in the Air, whither they moved after draining Reigelheimer's of what joys it had to offer, and at Peale's, where they went after wearying of Frolics in the Air, he was in the highest spirits. It was only occasionally that the recollection came to vex him that this could not last, that – since his Uncle Ira had played him false – he must return anon to the place whence he had come.

Why, in a city of all-night restaurants, these parties ever break up one cannot say, but a merciful Providence sees to it that they do, and just as Lord Dawlish was contemplating an eternity of the company of Nutty and his two companions, the end came. Miss Leonard said that she was tired. Her friend said that it was a shame to go home at dusk like this, but, if the party was going to be broken up, she supposed there was nothing else for it. Bill was too sleepy to say anything.

The Good Sport lived round the corner, and only required Lord Dawlish's escort for a couple of hundred yards. But Miss Leonard's hotel was in the neighbourhood of Washington

Square, and it was Nutty's pleasing task to drive her thither. Engaged thus, he received a shock that electrified him.

'That pal of yours,' said Miss Leonard, drowsily – she was half-asleep – 'what did you say his name was?'

'Chalmers, he told me. I only met him to-night.'

'Well, it isn't; it's something else. It' – Miss Leonard yawned – 'it's Lord something.'

'How do you mean, "Lord something"?'

'He's a lord – at least, he was when I met him in London.'

'Are you sure you met him in London?'

'Of course I'm sure. He was at that supper Captain Delaney gave at Oddy's. There can't be two men in England who dance like that!'

The recollection of Bill's performance stimulated Miss Leonard into a temporary wakefulness, and she giggled.

'He danced just the same way that night in London. I wish I could remember his name. I almost had it a dozen times to-night. It's something with a window in it.'

'A window?' Nutty's brain was a little fatigued and he felt himself unequal to grasping this. 'How do you mean, a window?'

'No, not a window – a door! I knew it was something about a house. I know now, his name's Lord Dawlish.'

Nutty's fatigue fell from him like a garment.

'It can't be!'

'It is.'

Miss Leonard's eyes had closed and she spoke in a muffled voice.

'Are you sure?'

'Mm-mm.'

'By gad!'

Nutty was wide awake now and full of inquiries; but his companion unfortunately was asleep, and he could not put them to her. A gentleman cannot prod a lady – and his guest, at that – in the ribs in order to wake her up and ask her questions. Nutty sat back and gave himself up to feverish thought.

He could think of no reason why Lord Dawlish should have come to America calling himself William Chalmers, but that was no reason why he should not have done so. And Daisy Leonard, who all along had remembered meeting him in London, had identified him.

Nutty was convinced. Arriving finally at Miss Leonard's hotel, he woke her up and saw her in at the door; then, telling the man to drive to the lodgings of his new friend, he urged his mind to rapid thought. He had decided as a first step in the following up of this matter to invite Bill down to Elizabeth's farm, and the thought occurred to him that this had better be done to-night, for he knew by experience that on the morning after these little jaunts he was seldom in the mood to seek people out and invite them to go anywhere.

All the way to the flat he continued to think, and it was wonderful what possibilities there seemed to be in this little scheme of courting the society of the man who had robbed him of his inheritance. He had worked on Bill's feelings so successfully as to elicit a loan of a million dollars, and was just proceeding to marry him to Elizabeth, when the cab stopped with the sudden sharpness peculiar to New York cabs, and he woke up, to find himself at his destination.

Bill was in bed when the bell rang, and received his late host in his pyjamas, wondering, as he did so, whether this was the New York custom, to foregather again after a party had been broken up, and chat till breakfast. But Nutty, it seemed, had come with a motive, not from a desire for more conversation.

'Sorry to disturb you, old man,' said Nutty. 'I looked in to tell you that I was going down to the country to-morrow. I wondered whether you would care to come and spend a day or two with us.'

Bill was delighted. This was better than he had hoped for. 'Rather!' he said. 'Thanks awfully!'

'There are plenty of trains in the afternoon,' said Nutty. 'I don't suppose either of us will feel like getting up early. I'll call for you here at half-past six, and we'll have an early dinner and catch the seven-fifteen, shall we? We live very simply, you know. You won't mind that?'

'My dear chap!'

'That's all right, then,' said Nutty, closing the door. 'Good night.'

9

ELIZABETH entered Nutty's room and, seating herself on the bed, surveyed him with a bright, quiet eye that drilled holes in her brother's uneasy conscience. This was her second visit to him that morning. She had come an hour ago, bearing breakfast on a tray, and had departed without saying a word. It was this uncanny silence of hers even more than the effects – which still lingered – of his revels in the metropolis that had interfered with Nutty's enjoyment of the morning meal. Never a hearty breakfaster, he had found himself under the influence of her wordless disapproval physically unable to consume the fried egg that confronted him. He had given it one look; then, endorsing the opinion which he had once heard a character in a play utter in somewhat similar circumstances – that there was nothing on earth so homely as an egg – he had covered it with a handkerchief and tried to pull himself round with hot tea. He was now smoking a sad cigarette and waiting for the blow to fall.

Her silence had puzzled him. Though he had tried to give her no opportunity of getting him alone on the previous evening when he had arrived at the farm with Lord Dawlish, he had fully expected that she would have broken in upon him with abuse and recrimination in the middle of the night. Yet she had not done this, nor had she spoken to him when bringing him his breakfast. These things found their explanation in Elizabeth's character, with which Nutty, though he had known her so long, was but imperfectly acquainted. Elizabeth had never been angrier with her brother, but an innate goodness of heart had prevented her falling upon him before he had had rest and refreshment.

She wanted to massacre him, but at the same time she told herself that the poor dear must be feeling very, very ill, and should have a reasonable respite before the slaughter commenced.

It was plain that in her opinion this respite had now lasted long enough. She looked over her shoulder to make sure that she had closed the door, then leaned a little forward and spoke.

'Now, Nutty!'

The wretched youth attempted bluster.

'What do you mean – "Now, Nutty"? What's the use of looking at a fellow like that and saying "Now, Nutty"? Where's the sense –'

His voice trailed off. He was not a very intelligent young man, but even he could see that his was not a position where righteous indignation could be assumed with any solid chance of success. As a substitute he tried pathos.

'Oo-oo, my head does ache!'

'I wish it would burst,' said his sister, unkindly.

'That's a nice thing to say to a fellow!'

'I'm sorry. I wouldn't have said it –'

'Oh, well!'

'Only I couldn't think of anything worse.'

It began to seem to Nutty that pathos was a bit of a failure too. As a last resort he fell back on silence. He wriggled as far down as he could beneath the sheets and breathed in a soft and wounded sort of way. Elizabeth took up the conversation.

'Nutty,' she said, 'I've struggled for years against the conviction that you were a perfect idiot. I've forced myself, against my better judgement, to try to look on you as sane, but now I give in. I can't believe you are responsible for your actions. Don't imagine that I am going to heap you with reproaches because you sneaked off to New York. I'm not even going to tell you what I thought of you for not sending me a telegram, letting me know where you were. I can understand all that. You were disappointed because Uncle Ira had not left you his money, and I suppose that was your way of working it off. If you had just run away and come back again with a headache, I'd have treated you like the Prodigal Son. But there are some things which are too much, and bringing a perfect stranger back with you for an indefinite period is one of them. I'm not saying anything against Mr Chalmers personally. I haven't had time to find out much about him, except that he's an

Englishman; but he looks respectable. Which, as he's a friend of yours, is more or less of a miracle.'

She raised her eyebrows as a faint moan of protest came from beneath the sheets.

'You surely,' she said, 'aren't going to suggest at this hour of the day, Nutty, that your friends aren't the most horrible set of pests outside a prison? Not that it's likely after all these months that they are outside a prison. You know perfectly well that while you were running round New York you collected the most pernicious bunch of rogues that ever fastened their talons into a silly child who ought never to have been allowed out without his nurse.' After which complicated insult Elizabeth paused for breath, and there was silence for a space.

'Well, as I was saying, I know nothing against this Mr Chalmers. Probably his finger-prints are in the Rogues' Gallery, and he is better known to the police as Jack the Blood, or something, but he hasn't shown that side of him yet. My point is that, whoever he is, I do not want him or anybody else coming and taking up his abode here while I have to be cook and housemaid too. I object to having a stranger on the premises spying out the nakedness of the land. I am sensitive about my honest poverty. So, darling Nutty, my precious Nutty, you poor boneheaded muddler, will you kindly think up at your earliest convenience some plan for politely ejecting this Mr Chalmers of yours from our humble home? – because if you don't, I'm going to have a nervous breakdown.'

And, completely restored to good humour by her own elo-quence, Elizabeth burst out laughing. It was a trait in her character which she had often lamented, that she could not succeed in keeping angry with anyone for more than a few minutes on end. Sooner or later some happy selection of a phrase of abuse would tickle her sense of humour, or the appear-ance of her victim would become too funny not to be laughed at. On the present occasion it was the ridiculous spectacle of Nutty cowering beneath the bedclothes that caused her wrath to evaporate. She made a weak attempt to recover it. She glared at Nutty, who at the sound of her laughter had emerged from under the clothes like a worm after a thunderstorm.

'I mean it,' she said. 'It really is too bad of you! You might have had some sense and a little consideration Ask yourself if we are in a position here to entertain visitors. Well, I'm going to make myself very unpopular with this Mr Chalmers of yours. By this evening he will be regarding me with utter loathing, for I am about to persecute him.'

'What do you mean?' asked Nutty, alarmed.

'I am going to begin by asking him to help me open one of the hives.'

'For goodness' sake!'

'After that I shall – with his assistance – transfer some honey. And after that – well, I don't suppose he will be alive by then. If he is, I shall make him wash the dishes for me. The least he can do, after swooping down on us like this, is to make himself useful.'

A cry of protest broke from the appalled Nutty, but Elizabeth did not hear it. She had left the room and was on her way downstairs.

Lord Dawlish was smoking an after-breakfast cigar in the grounds. It was a beautiful day, and a peaceful happiness had come upon him. He told himself that he had made progress. He was under the same roof as the girl he had deprived of her inheritance, and it should be simple to establish such friendly relations as would enable him to reveal his identity and ask her to reconsider her refusal to relieve him of a just share of her uncle's money. He had seen Elizabeth for only a short time on the previous night, but he had taken an immediate liking to her. There was something about the American girl, he reflected, which seemed to put a man at his ease, a charm and directness all her own. Yes, he liked Elizabeth, and he liked this dwelling-place of hers. He was quite willing to stay on here indefinitely.

Nature had done well by Flack's. The house itself was more pleasing to the eye than most of the houses in those parts, owing to the black and white paint which decorated it and an unconventional flattening and rounding of the roof. Nature, too, had made so many improvements that the general effect was unusually delightful.

Bill perceived Elizabeth coming toward him from the house.

69

He threw away his cigar and went to meet her. Seen by daylight, she was more attractive than ever. She looked so small and neat and wholesome, so extremely unlike Miss Daisy Leonard's friend. And such was the reaction from what might be termed his later Reigelheimer's mood that if he had been asked to define feminine charm in a few words, he would have replied without hesitation that it was the quality of being as different as possible in every way from the Good Sport. Elizabeth fulfilled this qualification. She was not only small and neat, but she had a soft voice to which it was a joy to listen.

'I was just admiring your place,' he said.

'Its appearance is the best part of it,' said Elizabeth. 'It is a deceptive place. The bay looks beautiful, but you can't bathe in it because of the jellyfish. The woods are lovely, but you daren't go near them because of the ticks.'

'Ticks?'

'They jump on you and suck your blood,' said Elizabeth, carelessly. 'And the nights are gorgeous, but you have to stay indoors after dusk because of the mosquitoes.' She paused to mark the effect of these horrors on her visitor. 'And then, of course,' she went on, as he showed no signs of flying to the house to pack his bag and catch the next train, 'the bees are always stinging you. I hope you are not afraid of bees, Mr Chalmers?'

'Rather not. Jolly little chaps!'

A gleam appeared in Elizabeth's eye.

'If you are so fond of them, perhaps you wouldn't mind coming and helping me open one of the hives?'

'Rather!'

'I'll go and fetch the things.'

She went into the house and ran up to Nutty's room, waking that sufferer from a troubled sleep.

'Nutty, he's bitten.'

Nutty sat up violently.

'Good gracious! What by?'

'You don't understand. What I meant was that I invited your Mr Chalmers to help me open a hive, and he said "Rather!" and is waiting to do it now. Be ready to say good-bye to him.

If he comes out of this alive, his first act, after bathing the wounds with ammonia, will be to leave us for ever.'

'But look here, he's a visitor –'

'Cheer up! He won't be much longer.'

'You can't let him in for a ghastly thing like opening a hive. When you made me do it that time I was picking stings out of myself for a week.'

'That was because you had been smoking. Bees dislike the smell of tobacco.'

'But this fellow may have been smoking.'

'He has just finished a strong cigar.'

'For Heaven's sake!'

'Good-bye, Nutty, dear; I mustn't keep him waiting.'

Lord Dawlish looked with interest at the various implements which she had collected when she rejoined him outside. He relieved her of the stool, the smoker, the cotton-waste, the knife, the screwdriver, and the queen-clipping cage.

'Let me carry these for you,' he said, 'unless you've hired a van.'

Elizabeth disapproved of this flippancy. It was out of place in one who should have been trembling at the prospect of doom.

'Don't you wear a veil for this sort of job?'

As a rule Elizabeth did. She had reached a stage of intimacy with her bees which rendered a veil a superfluous precaution, but until to-day she had never abandoned it. Her view of the matter was that, though the inhabitants of the hives were familiar and friendly with her by this time and recognized that she came among them without hostile intent, it might well happen that among so many thousands there might be one slow-witted enough and obtuse enough not to have grasped this fact. And in such an event a veil was better than any amount of explanations, for you cannot stick to pure reason when quarrelling with bees.

But to-day it had struck her that she could hardly protect herself in this way without offering a similar safeguard to her visitor, and she had no wish to hedge him about with safeguards.

'Oh, no,' she said, brightly; 'I'm not afraid of a few bees. Are you?'

'Rather not!'

'You know what to do if one of them flies at you?'

'Well, it would, anyway – what? What I mean to say is, I could leave most of the doing to the bee.'

Elizabeth was more disapproving than ever. This was mere bravado. She did not speak again until they reached the hives.

In the neighbourhood of the hives a vast activity prevailed. What, heard from afar, had been a pleasant murmur became at close quarters a menacing tumult. The air was full of bees – bees sallying forth for honey, bees returning with honey, bees trampling on each other's heels, bees pausing in mid-air to pass the time of day with rivals on competing lines of traffic. Blunt-bodied drones whizzed to and fro with a noise like miniature high-powered automobiles, as if anxious to convey the idea of being tremendously busy without going to the length of doing any actual work. One of these blundered into Lord Dawlish's face, and it pleased Elizabeth to observe that he gave a jump.

'Don't be afraid,' she said, 'it's only a drone. Drones have no stings.'

'They have hard heads, though. Here he comes again!'

'I suppose he smells your tobacco. A drone has thirty-seven thousand eight hundred nostrils, you know.'

'That gives him a sporting chance of smelling a cigar – what? I mean to say, if he misses with eight hundred of his nostrils he's apt to get it with the other thirty-seven thousand.'

Elizabeth was feeling annoyed with her bees. They resolutely declined to sting this young man. Bees flew past him, bees flew into him, bees settled upon his coat, bees paused questioningly in front of him, as who should say, 'What have we here?' but not a single bee molested him. Yet when Nutty, poor darling, went within a dozen yards of the hives he never failed to suffer for it. In her heart Elizabeth knew perfectly well that this was because Nutty, when in the presence of the bees, lost his head completely and behaved like an exaggerated version of Lady Wetherby's Dream of Psyche, whereas Bill maintained an easy calm; but at the moment she put the phenomenon down to that inexplicable cussedness which does so much to exasperate the human race, and it fed her annoyance with her unbidden guest.

Without commenting on his last remark, she took the smoker from him and set to work. She inserted in the fire-chamber a handful of the cotton-waste and set fire to it; then with a preliminary puff or two of the bellows to make sure that the conflagration had not gone out, she aimed the nozzle at the front door of the hive.

The results were instantaneous. One or two bee-policemen, who were doing fixed point-duty near the opening, scuttled hastily back into the hive; and from within came a muffled buzzing as other bees, all talking at once, worried the perplexed officials with foolish questions, a buzzing that became less muffled and more pronounced as Elizabeth lifted the edge of the cover and directed more smoke through the crack. This done, she removed the cover, set it down on the grass beside her, lifted the super-cover and applied more smoke, and raised her eyes to where Bill stood watching. His face wore a smile of pleased interest.

Elizabeth's irritation became painful. She resented his smile. She hung the smoker on the side of the hive.

'The stool, please, and the screw-driver.'

She seated herself beside the hive and began to loosen the outside section. Then taking the brood-frame by the projecting ends, she pulled it out and handed it to her companion. She did it as one who plays an ace of trumps.

'Would you mind holding this, Mr Chalmers?'

This was the point in the ceremony at which the wretched Nutty had broken down absolutely, and not inexcusably, considering the severity of the test. The surface of the frame was black with what appeared at first sight to be a thick, bubbling fluid of some sort, pouring viscously to and fro as if some hidden fire had been lighted beneath it. Only after a closer inspection was it apparent to the lay eye that this seeming fluid was in reality composed of mass upon mass of bees. They shoved and writhed and muttered and jostled, for all the world like a collection of home-seeking City men trying to secure standing room on the Underground at half-past five in the afternoon.

Nutty, making this discovery, had emitted one wild yell, dropped the frame, and started at full speed for the house, his retreat expedited by repeated stings from the nervous bees. Bill, more prudent, remained absolutely motionless. He eyed the seething frame with interest, but without apparent panic.

'I want you to help me here, Mr Chalmers. You have stronger wrists than I have. I will tell you what to do. Hold the frame tightly.'

'I've got it.'

'Jerk it down as sharply as you can to within a few inches of the door, and then jerk it up again. You see, that shakes them off.'

'It would me,' agreed Bill, cordially, 'if I were a bee.'

Elizabeth had the feeling that she had played her ace of trumps and by some miracle lost the trick. If this grisly operation did not daunt the man, nothing, not even the transferring of honey, would. She watched him as he raised the frame and jerked it down with a strong swiftness which her less powerful wrists had never been able to achieve. The bees tumbled off in a dense shower, asking questions to the last; then, sighting the familiar entrance to the hive, they bustled in without waiting to investigate the cause of the earthquake.

Lord Dawlish watched them go with a kindly interest.

'It has always been a mystery to me,' he said, 'why they never seem to think of manhandling the Johnny who does that to them. They don't seem able to connect cause and effect. I suppose the only way they can figure it out is that the bottom has suddenly dropped out of everything, and they are so busy lighting out for home that they haven't time to go to the root of things. But it's a ticklish job, for all that, if you're not used to it. I know when I first did it I shut my eyes and wondered whether they would bury my remains or cremate them.'

'When you first did it?' Elizabeth was staring at him blankly. 'Have you done it before?'

Her voice shook. Bill met her gaze frankly.

'Done it before? Rather! Thousands of times. You see, I spent a year on a bee-farm once, learning the business.'

For a moment mortification was the only emotion of which Elizabeth was conscious. She felt supremely ridiculous. For this she had schemed and plotted – to give a practised expert the opportunity of doing what he had done a thousand times before!

And then her mood changed in a flash. Nature has decreed that there are certain things in life which shall act as hoops of steel, grappling the souls of the elect together. Golf is one of these; a mutual love of horseflesh another; but the greatest of all is bees. Between two beekeepers there can be no strife. Not even a tepid hostility can mar their perfect communion.

The petty enmities which life raises to be barriers between man and man and between man and woman vanish once it is revealed to them that they are linked by this great bond. Envy, malice, hatred, and all uncharitableness disappear, and they look into each other's eyes and say 'My brother!'

The effect of Bill's words on Elizabeth was revolutionary. They crashed through her dislike, scattering it like an explosive shell. She had resented this golden young man's presence at the farm. She had thought him in the way. She had objected to his becoming aware that she did such prosaic tasks as cooking and washing-up. But now her whole attitude toward him was changed. She reflected that he was there. He could stay there as long as he liked, the longer the better.

'You have really kept bees?'

'Not actually kept them, worse luck! I couldn't raise the capital. You see, money was a bit tight –'

'I know,' said Elizabeth, sympathetically. 'Money is like that, isn't it?'

'The general impression seemed to be that I should be foolish to try anything so speculative as beekeeping, so it fell through. Some very decent old boys got me another job.'

'What job?'

'Secretary to a club.'

'In London, of course?'

'Yes.'

'And all the time you wanted to be in the country keeping bees!'

Elizabeth could hardly control her voice, her pity was so great.

'I should have liked it,' said Bill, wistfully. 'London's all right, but I love the country. My ambition would be to have a whacking big farm, a sort of ranch, miles away from anywhere –'

He broke off. This was not the first time he had caught himself forgetting how his circumstances had changed in the past few weeks. It was ridiculous to be telling hard-luck stories about not being able to buy a farm, when he had the wherewithal to buy dozens of farms. It took a lot of getting used to, this business of being a millionaire.

'That's my ambition too,' said Elizabeth, eagerly. This was the very first time she had met a congenial spirit. Nutty's views on farming and the Arcadian life generally were saddening to an enthusiast. 'If I had the money I should get an enormous farm, and in the summer I should borrow all the children I could find, and take them out to it and let them wallow in it.'

'Wouldn't they do a lot of damage?'

'I shouldn't mind. I should be too rich to worry about the damage. If they ruined the place beyond repair I'd go and buy another.' She laughed. 'It isn't so impossible as it sounds. I came very near being able to do it.' She paused for a moment, but went on almost at once. After all, if you cannot confide your intimate troubles to a fellow bee-lover, to whom can you confide them? 'An uncle of mine –'

Bill felt himself flushing. He looked away from her. He had a sense of almost unbearable guilt, as if he had just done some particularly low crime and was contemplating another.

'–An uncle of mine would have left me enough money to buy all the farms I wanted, only an awful person, an English lord I wonder if you have heard of him? – Lord Dawlish – got hold of uncle somehow and induced him to make a will leaving all the money to him.'

She looked at Bill for sympathy, and was touched to see that he was crimson with emotion. He must be a perfect dear to take other people's misfortunes to heart like that.

'I don't know how he managed it,' she went on. 'He must

have worked and plotted and schemed, for Uncle Ira wasn't a weak sort of man whom you could do what you liked with. He was very obstinate. But, anyway, this Lord Dawlish suc- ceeded in doing it somehow, and then' – her eyes blazed at the recollection – 'he had the insolence to write to me through his lawyers offering me half. I suppose he was hoping to satisfy his conscience. Naturally I refused it.'

'But – but – but why?'

'Why! Why did I refuse it? Surely you don't think I was going to accept charity from the man who had cheated me?'

'But – but perhaps he didn't mean it like that. What I mean to say is – as charity, you know.'

'He did! But don't let's talk of it any more. It makes me angry to think of him, and there's no use spoiling a lovely day like this by getting angry.'

Bill sighed. He had never dreamed before that it could be so difficult to give money away. He was profoundly glad that he had not revealed his identity, as he had been on the very point of doing just when she began her remarks. He understood now why that curt refusal had come in answer to his lawyer's letter. Well, there was nothing to do but wait and hope that time might accomplish something.

'What do you want me to do next?' he said. 'Why did you open the hive? Did you want to take a look at the queen?'

Elizabeth hesitated. She blushed with pure shame. She had had but one motive in opening the hive, and that had been to annoy him. She scorned to take advantage of the loophole he had provided. Beekeeping is a freemasonry. A beekeeper can- not deceive a brother-mason.

She faced him bravely.

'I didn't want to take a look at anything, Mr Chalmers. I opened that hive because I wanted you to drop the frame, as my brother did, and get stung, as he was; because I thought that would drive you away, because I thought then that I didn't want you down here. I'm ashamed of myself, and I don't know where I'm getting the nerve to tell you this. I hope you will stay on – on and on and on.'

Bill was aghast.

'Good Lord! If I'm in the way –'

'You aren't in the way.'

'But you said –'

'But don't you see that it's so different now? I didn't know then that you were fond of bees. You must stay, if my telling you hasn't made you feel that you want to catch the next train. You will save our lives – mine and Nutty's too. Oh, dear, you're hesitating! You're trying to think up some polite way of getting out of the place! You mustn't go, Mr Chalmers; you simply must stay. There aren't any mosquitoes, no jellyfish – nothing! At least, there are; but what do they matter? You don't mind them. Do you play golf?'

'Yes.'

'There are links here. You can't go until you've tried them. What is your handicap?'

'Plus two.'

'So is mine.'

'By Jove! Really?'

Elizabeth looked at him, her eyes dancing.

'Why, we're practically twin souls, Mr Chalmers! Tell me, I know your game is nearly perfect, but if you have a fault, is it a tendency to putt too hard?'

'Why, by Jove – yes, it is!'

'I knew it. Something told me. It's the curse of my life too! Well, after that you can't go away.'

'But if I'm in the way –'

'In the way! Mr Chalmers, will you come in now and help me wash the breakfast things?'

'Rather!' said Lord Dawlish.

10

In the days that followed their interrupted love-scene at Reigelheimer's Restaurant that night of Lord Dawlish's unfortunate encounter with the tray-bearing waiter, Dudley Pickering's behaviour had perplexed Claire Fenwick. She had taken it for granted that next day at the latest he would resume the offer of his hand, heart, and automobiles. But time passed and he made no move in that direction. Of limousine bodies, carburettors, spark-plugs, and inner tubes he spoke with freedom and eloquence, but the subject of love and marriage he avoided absolutely. His behaviour was inexplicable.

Claire was piqued. She was in the position of a hostess who has swept and garnished her house against the coming of a guest and waits in vain for that guest's arrival. She made up her mind what to do when Dudley Pickering proposed to her next time, and thereby, it seemed to her, had removed all difficulties in the way of that proposal. She little knew her Pickering!

Dudley Pickering was not a self-starter in the motordrome of love. He needed cranking. He was that most unpromising of matrimonial material, a shy man with a cautious disposition. If he overcame his shyness, caution applied the foot-brake. If he succeeded in forgetting caution, shyness shut off the gas. At Reigelheimer's some miracle had made him not only reckless but un-self-conscious. Possibly the Dream of Psyche had gone to his head. At any rate, he had been on the very verge of proposing to Claire when the interruption had occurred, and in bed that night, reviewing the affair, he had been appalled at the narrowness of his escape from taking a definite step. Except in the way of business, he was a man who hated definite steps. He never accepted even a dinner invitation without subsequent doubts and remorse. The consequence was that, in the days that followed the Reigelheimer episode, what Lord Wetherby would have called the lamp of love burned rather low in Mr Pickering, as if the acetylene were running out. He still admired Claire intensely and experienced disturbing emotions when he beheld her perfect tonneau and wonderful headlights; but he regarded her with a cautious fear. Although he sometimes dreamed sentimentally of marriage in the abstract, of actual marriage, of marriage with a flesh-and-blood individual, of marriage that involved clergymen and 'Voices that Breathe o'er Eden,' and giggling bridesmaids and cake, Dudley Pickering was afraid with a terror that woke him sweating in the night. His shyness shrank from the ceremony, his caution jibbed at the mysteries of married life. So his attitude toward Claire, the only girl who had succeeded in bewitching him into the opening words of an actual proposal, was a little less cordial and affectionate than if she had been a rival automobile manufacturer.

Matters were in this state when Lady Wetherby, who, having danced classical dances for three months without a break, required a rest, shifted her camp to the house which she had rented for the summer at Brookport, Long Island, taking with her Algie, her husband, the monkey Eustace, and Claire and Mr Pickering, her guests. The house was a large one, capable of receiving a big party, but she did not wish to entertain on an ambitious scale. The only other guest she proposed to put up was Roscoe Sherriff, her press agent, who was to come down as soon as he could get away from his metropolitan duties.

It was a pleasant and romantic place, the estate which Lady Wetherby had rented. Standing on a hill, the house looked down through green trees on the gleaming waters of the bay. Smooth lawns and shady walks it had, and rustic seats beneath spreading cedars. Yet for all its effect on Dudley Pickering it might have been a gasworks. He roamed the smooth lawns with Claire, and sat with her on the rustic benches and talked guardedly of lubricating oil. There were moments when Claire was almost impelled to forfeit whatever chance she might have had of becoming mistress of thirty million dollars and a flourishing business, for the satisfaction of administering just one whole-hearted slap on his round and thinly-covered head.

And then Roscoe Sherriff came down, and Dudley Pickering, who for days had been using all his resolution to struggle against the siren, suddenly found that there was no siren to struggle against. No sooner had the press agent appeared than Claire deserted him shamelessly and absolutely. She walked with Roscoe Sherriff. Mr Pickering experienced the discomfiting emotions of the man who pushes violently against an abruptly-yielding door, or treads heavily on the top stair where there is no top stair. He was shaken, and the clamlike stolidity which he had assumed as protection gave way.

Night had descended upon Brookport. Eustace, the monkey,

was in his little bed; Lord Wetherby in the smoking-room. It was Sunday, the day of rest. Dinner was over, and the remainder of the party were gathered in the drawing-room, with the exception of Mr Pickering, who was smoking a cigar on the porch. A full moon turned Long Island into a fairyland.

Gloom had settled upon Dudley Pickering and he smoked sadly. All rather stout automobile manufacturers are sad when there is a full moon. It makes them feel lonely. It stirs their hearts to thoughts of love. Marriage loses its terrors for them, and they think wistfully of hooking some fair woman up the back and buying her hats. Such was the mood of Mr Pickering, when through the dimness of the porch there appeared a white shape, moving softly toward him.

'Is that you, Mr Pickering?'

Claire dropped into the seat beside him. From the drawing-room came the soft tinkle of a piano. The sound blended harmoniously with the quiet peace of the night. Mr Pickering let his cigar go out and clutched the sides of his chair

> Oi'll – er – sing thee saw-ongs ov Arrabee,
>   Und – ah ta-ales of farrr Cash-mee-eere,
> Wi-ild tales to che-eat thee ovasigh
>   Und charrrrm thee to-oo a tear-er.

Claire gave a little sigh.

'What a beautiful voice Mr Sherriff has!'

Dudley Pickering made no reply. He thought Roscoe Sherriff had a beastly voice. He resented Roscoe Sherriff's voice. He objected to Roscoe Sherriff's polluting this fair night with his cacophony.

'Don't you think so, Mr Pickering?'

'Uh-huh.'

'That doesn't sound very enthusiastic. Mr Pickering, I want you to tell me something. Have I done anything to offend you?'

Mr Pickering started violently.

'Eh?'

'I have seen so little of you these last few days. A little while ago we were always together, having such interesting talks. But lately it has seemed to me that you have been avoiding me.'

81

A feeling of helplessness swept over Mr Pickering. He was vaguely conscious of a sense of being treated unjustly, of there being a flaw in Claire's words somewhere if he could only find it, but the sudden attack had deprived him of the free and unfettered use of his powers of reasoning. He gurgled wordlessly, and Claire went on, her low, sad voice mingling with the moonlight in a manner that caused thrills to run up and down his spine. He felt paralyzed. Caution urged him to make some excuse and follow it with a bolt to the drawing-room, but he was physically incapable of taking the excellent advice. Sometimes when you are out in your Pickering Gem or your Pickering Giant the car hesitates, falters, and stops dead, and your chauffeur, having examined the carburettor, turns to you and explains the phenomenon in these words: 'The mixture is too rich.' So was it with Mr Pickering now. The moonlight alone might not have held him; Claire's voice alone might not have held him; but against the two combined he was powerless. The mixture was too rich. He sat and breathed a little stertorously, and there came to him that conviction that comes to all of us now and then, that we are at a crisis of our careers and that the moment through which we are living is a moment big with fate.

The voice in the drawing-room stopped. Having sung songs of Araby and tales of far Cashmere, Mr Roscoe Sherriff was refreshing himself with a comic paper. But Lady Wetherby, seated at the piano, still touched the keys softly, and the sound increased the richness of the mixture which choked Dudley Pickering's spiritual carburettor. It is not fair that a rather stout manufacturer should be called upon to sit in the moonlight while a beautiful girl, to the accompaniment of soft music, reproaches him with having avoided her.

'I should be so sorry, Mr Pickering, if I had done anything to make a difference between us –'

'Eh?' said Mr Pickering.

'I have so few real friends over here.'

Claire's voice trembled.

'I – I get a little lonely, a little homesick sometimes –'

She paused, musing, and a spasm of pity rent the bosom

beneath Dudley Pickering's ample shirt. There was a buzzing in his ears and a lump choked his throat.

'Of course, I am loving the life here. I think America's wonderful, and nobody could be kinder than Lady Wetherby. But – I miss my home. It's the first time I have been away for so long. I feel very far away sometimes. There are only three of us at home: my mother, myself, and my little brother – little Percy.'

Her voice trembled again as she spoke the last two words, and it was possibly this that caused Mr Pickering to visualize Percy as a sort of little Lord Fauntleroy, his favourite character in English literature. He had a vision of a small, delicate, wistful child pining away for his absent sister. Consumptive probably. Or curvature of the spine.

He found Claire's hand in his. He supposed dully he must have reached out for it. Soft and warm it lay there, while the universe paused breathlessly. And then from the semi-darkness beside him there came the sound of a stifled sob, and his fingers closed as if someone had touched a button.

'We have always been such chums. He is only ten – such a dear boy! He must be missing me – '

She stopped, and simultaneously Dudley Pickering began to speak.

There is this to be said for your shy, cautious man, that on the rare occasions when he does tap the vein of eloquence that vein becomes a geyser. It was as if after years of silence and monosyllables Dudley Pickering was endeavouring to restore the average.

He began by touching on his alleged neglect and avoidance of Claire. He called himself names and more names. He plumbed the depth of repentance and remorse. Proceeding from this, he eulogized her courage, the pluck with which she presented a smiling face to the world while tortured inwardly by separation from her little brother Percy. He then turned to his own feelings.

But there are some things which the historian should hold sacred, some things which he should look on as proscribed material for his pen, and the actual words of a stout manufacturer of automobiles proposing marriage in the moonlight fall into this class. It is enough to say that Dudley Pickering was definite. He left no room for doubt as to his meaning.

'Dudley!'

She was in his arms. He was embracing her. She was his – the latest model, self-starting, with limousine body and all the newest. No, no, his mind was wandering. She was his, this divine girl, this queen among women, this –

From the drawing-room Roscoe Sherriff's voice floated out in unconscious comment –

> Good-bye, boys!
>   I'm going to be married to-morrow.
> Good-bye, boys!
>   I'm going from sunshine to sorrow.
> No more sitting up till broad daylight.

Did a momentary chill cool the intensity of Dudley Pickering's ardour? If so he overcame it instantly. He despised Roscoe Sherriff. He flattered himself that he had shown Roscoe Sherriff pretty well who was who and what was what.

They would have a wonderful wedding – dozens of clergymen, scores of organs playing 'The Voice that Breathed o'er Eden,' platoons of bridesmaids, wagonloads of cake. And then they would go back to Detroit and live happy ever after. And it might be that in time to come there would be given to them little runabouts.

> I'm going to a life
> Of misery and strife,
> So good-bye, boys!

Hang Roscoe Sherriff! What did he know about it! Confound him! Dudley Pickering turned a deaf ear to the song and wallowed in his happiness.

Claire walked slowly down the moonlit drive. She had removed herself from her Dudley's embraces, for she wished to be alone, to think. The engagement had been announced. All that part of it was over – Dudley's stammering speech, the unrestrained delight of Polly Wetherby, the facetious rendering of 'The Wedding Glide' on the piano by Roscoe Sherriff, and it now remained for her to try to discover a way of conveying the news to Bill.

It had just struck her that, though she knew that Bill was in America, she had not his address.

What was she to do? She must tell him. Otherwise it might quite easily happen that they might meet in New York when she returned there. She pictured the scene. She saw herself walking with Dudley Pickering. Along came Bill. 'Claire, darling!' . . . Heavens, what would Dudley think? It would be too awful! She couldn't explain. No, somehow or other, even if she put detectives on his trail, she must find him, and be off with the old love now that she was on with the new.

She reached the gate and leaned over it. And as she did so someone in the shadow of a tall tree spoke her name. A man came into the light, and she saw that it was Lord Dawlish.

II

LORD DAWLISH had gone for a moonlight walk that night because, like Claire, he wished to be alone to think. He had fallen with a pleasant ease and smoothness into the rather curious life lived at Elizabeth Boyd's bee-farm. A liking for picnics had lingered in him from boyhood, and existence at Flack's was one prolonged picnic. He found that he had a natural aptitude for the more muscular domestic duties, and his energy in this direction enchanted Nutty, who before his advent had had a monopoly of these tasks.

Nor was this the only aspect of the situation that pleased Nutty. When he had invited Bill to the farm he had had a vague hope that good might come of it, but he had never dreamed that things would turn out as well as they promised to do, or that such a warm and immediate friendship would spring up between his sister and the man who had diverted the family fortune into his own pocket. Bill and Elizabeth were getting on splendidly. They were together all the time – walking, golfing, attending to the numerous needs of the bees, or sitting on the porch. Nutty's imagination began to run away with him. He seemed to smell the scent of orange-blossoms, to hear the joyous pealing of church bells – in fact, with the difference that it was not his own wedding that he was anticipating, he had begun to take very much the same view of the future that was about to come to Dudley Pickering.

Elizabeth would have been startled and embarrassed if she could have read his thoughts, for they might have suggested to her that she was becoming a great deal fonder of Bill than the shortness of their acquaintance warranted. But though she did not fail to observe the strangeness of her brother's manner, she traced it to another source than the real one. Nutty had a habit of starting back and removing himself when, entering the porch, he perceived that Bill and his sister were already seated there. His own impression on such occasions was that he was behaving with consummate tact. Elizabeth supposed that he had had some sort of a spasm.

Lord Dawlish, if he had been able to diagnose correctly the almost paternal attitude which had become his host's normal manner these days, would have been equally embarrassed but less startled, for conscience had already suggested to him from time to time that he had been guilty of a feeling toward Elizabeth warmer than any feeling that should come to an engaged man. Lying in bed at the end of his first week at the farm, he reviewed the progress of his friendship with her, and was amazed at the rapidity with which it had grown.

He could not conceal it from himself – Elizabeth appealed to him. Being built on a large scale himself, he had always been attracted by small women. There was a smallness, a daintiness, a liveliness about Elizabeth that was almost irresistible. She was so capable, so cheerful in spite of the fact that she was having a hard time. And then their minds seemed to blend so remarkably. There were no odd corners to be smoothed away. Never in his life had he felt so supremely at his ease with one of the opposite sex. He loved Claire – he drove that fact home almost angrily to himself – but he was forced to admit that he had always been aware of something in the nature of a barrier between them. Claire was querulous at times, and always a little too apt to take offence. He had never been able to talk to her with that easy freedom that Elizabeth invited. Talking to Elizabeth was like talking to an attractive version of oneself. It was a thing to be done with perfect confidence, without any of that apprehension which Claire inspired lest the next remark might prove the spark to cause an explosion. But Claire was the girl he loved – there must be no mistake about that.

He came to the conclusion that the key to the situation was the fact that Elizabeth was American. He had read so much of the American girl, her unaffectedness, her genius for easy comradeship. Well, this must be what the writer fellows meant. He had happened upon one of those delightful friendships without any suspicion of sex in them of which the American girl had the monopoly. Yes, that must be it. It was a comforting explanation. It accounted for his feeling at a loose end whenever he was away from Elizabeth for as much as half an hour. It accounted for the fact that they understood each other so well. It accounted for everything so satisfactorily that he was able to get to sleep that night after all.

But next morning – for his conscience was one of those persistent consciences – he began to have doubts again. Nothing clings like a suspicion in the mind of a conscientious young man that he has been allowing his heart to stray from its proper anchorage.

Could it be that he was behaving badly toward Claire? The thought was unpleasant, but he could not get rid of it. He extracted Claire's photograph from his suit-case and gazed solemnly upon it.

At first he was shocked to find that it only succeeded in convincing him that Elizabeth was quite the most attractive girl he ever had met. The photographer had given Claire rather a severe look. He had told her to moisten the lips with the tip of the tongue and assume a pleasant smile, with the result that she seemed to glare. She had a rather markedly aggressive look, queenly perhaps, but not very comfortable.

But there is no species of self-hypnotism equal to that of a man who gazes persistently at a photograph with the preconceived idea that he is in love with the original of it. Little by little Bill found that the old feeling began to return. He persevered. By the end of a quarter of an hour he had almost succeeded in capturing anew that first fine careless rapture which, six months ago, had caused him to propose to Claire and walk on air when she accepted him.

He continued the treatment throughout the day, and by dinner-time had arranged everything with his conscience in the most satisfactory manner possible. He loved Claire with a passionate fervour; he liked Elizabeth very much indeed. He submitted this diagnosis to conscience, and conscience graciously approved and accepted it.

It was Sunday that day. That helped. There is nothing like Sunday in a foreign country for helping a man to sentimental thoughts of the girl he has left behind him elsewhere. And the fact that there was a full moon clinched it. Bill was enabled to go for an after-dinner stroll in a condition of almost painful loyalty to Claire.

From time to time, as he walked along the road, he took out the photograph and did some more gazing. The last occasion on which he did this was just as he emerged from the shadow of a large tree that stood by the roadside, and a gush of rich emotion rewarded him.

'Claire!' he murmured.

An exclamation at his elbow caused him to look up. There, leaning over a gate, the light of the moon falling on her beautiful face, stood Claire herself!

12

In trying interviews, as in sprint races, the start is everything. It was the fact that she recovered more quickly from her astonishment that enabled Claire to dominate her scene with Bill. She had the advantage of having a less complicated astonishment to recover from, for, though it was a shock to see him there when she had imagined that he was in New York, it was not nearly such a shock as it was to him to see her here when he had imagined that she was in England. She had adjusted her brain to the situation while he was still gaping.

'Well, Bill?'

This speech in itself should have been enough to warn Lord Dawlish of impending doom. As far as love, affection, and tenderness are concerned, a girl might just as well hit a man with an axe as say 'Well, Bill?' to him when they have met unexpectedly in the moonlight after long separation. But Lord Dawlish was too shattered by surprise to be capable of observing *nuances*. If his love had ever waned or faltered, as conscience had suggested earlier in the day, it was at full blast now.

'Claire!' he cried.

He was moving to take her in his arms, but she drew back.

'No, really, Bill!' she said; and this time it did filter through into his disordered mind that all was not well. A man who is a good deal dazed at the moment may fail to appreciate a remark like 'Well, Bill?' but for a girl to draw back and say, 'No, really, Bill!' in a tone not exactly of loathing, but certainly of pained aversion, is a deliberately unfriendly act. The three short words, taken in conjunction with the movement, brought him up with as sharp a turn as if she had punched him in the eye.

'Claire! What's the matter?'

She looked at him steadily. She looked at him with a sort of queenly woodenness, as if he were behind a camera with a velvet bag over his head and had just told her to moisten the lips with the tip of the tongue. Her aspect staggered Lord Dawlish. A cursory inspection of his conscience showed nothing but purity and whiteness, but he must have done something, or she would not be staring at him like this.

'I don't understand!' was the only remark that occurred to him.

'Are you sure?'

'What do you mean?'

'I was at Reigelheimer's Restaurant – Ah!'

The sudden start which Lord Dawlish had given at the

opening words of her sentence justified the concluding word. Innocent as his behaviour had been that night at Reigelheimer's, he had been glad at the time that he had not been observed. It now appeared that he had been observed, and it seemed to him that Long Island suddenly flung itself into a whirling dance. He heard Claire speaking a long way off: 'I was there with Lady Wetherby. It was she who invited me to come to America. I went to the restaurant to see her dance – and I saw you!'

With a supreme effort Bill succeeded in calming down the excited landscape. He willed the trees to stop dancing, and they came reluctantly to a standstill. The world ceased to swim and flicker.

'Let me explain,' he said.

The moment he had said the words he wished he could recall them. Their substance was right enough; it was the sound of them that was wrong. They sounded like a line from a farce, where the erring husband has been caught by the masterful wife. They were ridiculous. Worse than being merely ridiculous, they created an atmosphere of guilt and evasion.

'Explain! How can you explain? It is impossible to explain. I saw you with my own eyes making an exhibition of yourself with a horrible creature in salmon-pink. I'm not asking you who she is. I'm not questioning you about your relations with her at all. I don't care who she was. The mere fact that you were at a public restaurant with a person of that kind is enough. No doubt you think I am making a great deal of fuss about a very ordinary thing. You consider that it is a man's privilege to do these things, if he can do them without being found out. But it ended everything so far as I am concerned. Am I unreasonable? I don't think so. You steal off to America, thinking I am in England, and behave like this. How could you do that if you really loved me? It's the deceit of it that hurts me.'

Lord Dawlish drew in a few breaths of pure Long Island air, but he did not speak. He felt helpless. If he were to be allowed to withdraw into the privacy of the study and wrap a cold, wet towel about his forehead and buckle down to it, he knew that he could draft an excellent and satisfactory explanation of his presence at Reigelheimer's with the Good Sport. But to do it on the spur of the moment like this was beyond him.

Claire was speaking again. She had paused for a while after her recent speech, in order to think of something else to say; and during this pause had come to her mind certain excerpts from one of those admirable articles on love, by Luella Delia Philpotts, which do so much to boost the reading public of the United States into the higher planes. She had read it that afternoon in the Sunday paper, and it came back to her now.

'I may be hypersensitive,' she said, dropping her voice from the accusatory register to the lower tones of pathos, 'but I have such high ideals of love. There can be no true love where there is not perfect trust. Trust is to love what – '

She paused again. She could not remember just what Luella Delia Philpotts had said trust was to love. It was something extremely neat, but it had slipped her memory.

'A woman has the right to expect the man she is about to marry to regard their troth as a sacred obligation that shall keep him as pure as a young knight who has dedicated himself to the quest of the Holy Grail. And I find you in a public restaurant, dancing with a creature with yellow hair, upsetting waiters, and staggering about with pats of butter all over you.'

Here a sense of injustice stung Lord Dawlish. It was true that after his regrettable collision with Heinrich, the waiter, he had discovered butter upon his person, but it was only one pat. Claire had spoken as if he had been festooned with butter.

'I am not angry with you, only disappointed. What has happened has shown me that you do not really love me, not as I think of love. Oh, I know that when we are together you think you do, but absence is the test. Absence is the acid-test of love that separates the base metal from the true. After what has happened, we can't go on with our engagement. It would be farcical. I could never feel that way toward you again. We shall always be friends, I hope. But as for love – love is not a machine. It cannot be shattered and put together again.'

She turned and began to walk up the drive. Hanging over the top of the gate like a wet sock, Lord Dawlish watched her go.

The interview was over, and he could not think of one single thing to say. Her white dress made a patch of light in the shadows. She moved slowly, as if weighed down by sad thoughts, like one who, as Luella Delia Philpotts beautifully puts it, paces with measured step behind the coffin of a murdered heart. The bend of the drive hid her from his sight.

About twenty minutes later Dudley Pickering, smoking sentimentally in the darkness hard by the porch, received a shock. He was musing tenderly on his Claire, who was assisting him in the process by singing in the drawing-room, when he was aware of a figure, the sinister figure of a man who, pressed against the netting of the porch, stared into the lighted room beyond.

Dudley Pickering's first impulse was to stride briskly up to the intruder, tap him on the shoulder, and ask him what the devil he wanted; but a second look showed him that the other was built on too ample a scale to make this advisable. He was a large, fit-looking intruder.

Mr Pickering was alarmed. There had been the usual epidemic of burglaries that season. Houses had been broken into, valuable possessions removed. In one case a negro butler had been struck over the head with a gas-pipe and given a headache. In these circumstances, it was unpleasant to find burly strangers looking in at windows.

'Hi!' cried Mr Pickering.

The intruder leaped a foot. It had not occurred to Lord Dawlish, when in an access of wistful yearning he had decided to sneak up to the house in order to increase his anguish by one last glimpse of Claire, that other members of the household might be out in the grounds. He was just thinking sorrowfully, as he listened to the music, how like his own position was to that of the hero of Tennyson's *Maud* – a poem to which he was greatly addicted, when Mr Pickering's 'Hi!' came out of nowhere and hit him like a torpedo.

He turned in agitation. Mr Pickering having prudently elected to stay in the shadows, there was no one to be seen. It was as if the voice of conscience had shouted 'Hi!' at him. He was just wondering if he had imagined the whole thing, when he perceived the red glow of a cigar and beyond it a shadowy form.

It was not the fact that he was in an equivocal position, staring into a house which did not belong to him, with his feet on somebody else's private soil, that caused Bill to act as he did. It was the fact that at that moment he was not feeling equal to conversation with anybody on any subject whatsoever. It did not occur to him that his behaviour might strike a nervous stranger as suspicious. All he aimed at was the swift removal of himself from a spot infested by others of his species. He ran, and Mr Pickering, having followed him with the eye of fear, went rather shakily into the house, his brain whirling with professional cracksmen and gas pipes and assaulted butlers, to relate his adventure.

'A great, hulking, ruffianly sort of fellow glaring in at the window,' said Mr Pickering. 'I shouted at him and he ran like a rabbit.'

'Gee! Must have been one of the gang that's been working down here,' said Roscoe Sherriff. 'There might be a quarter of a column in that, properly worked, but I guess I'd better wait until he actually does bust the place.'

'We must notify the police!'

'Notify the police, and have them butt in and stop the thing and kill a good story!' There was honest amazement in the Press-agent's voice. 'Let me tell you, it isn't so easy to get publicity these days that you want to go out of your way to stop it!'

Mr Pickering was appalled. A dislike of this man, which had grown less vivid since his scene with Claire, returned to him with redoubled force.

'Why, we may all be murdered in our beds!' he cried.

'Front-page stuff!' said Roscoe Sherriff, with gleaming eyes. 'And three columns at least. Fine!'

It might have consoled Lord Dawlish somewhat, as he lay awake that night, to have known that the man who had taken Claire from him – though at present he was not aware of such a man's existence – also slept ill.

13

LADY WETHERBY sat in her room, writing letters. The rest of the household were variously employed. Roscoe Sherriff was prowling about the house, brooding on campaigns of publicity. Dudley Pickering was walking in the grounds with Claire. In a little shack in the woods that adjoined the high-road, which he had converted into a temporary studio, Lord Wetherby was working on a picture which he proposed to call 'Innocence', a study of a small Italian child he had discovered in Washington Square. Lady Wetherby, who had been taken to see the picture, had suggested 'The Black Hand's Newest Recruit' as a better title than the one selected by the artist.

It is a fact to be noted that of the entire household only Lady Wetherby could fairly be described as happy. It took very little to make Lady Wetherby happy. Fine weather, good food, and a complete abstention from classical dancing – give her these and she asked no more. She was, moreover, delighted at Claire's engagement. It seemed to her, for she had no knowledge of the existence of Lord Dawlish, a genuine manifestation of Love's Young Dream. She liked Dudley Pickering and she was devoted to Claire. It made her happy to think that it was she who had brought them together.

But of the other members of the party, Dudley Pickering was unhappy because he feared that burglars were about to raid the house; Roscoe Sherriff because he feared they were not; Claire because, now that the news of the engagement was out, it seemed to be everybody's aim to leave her alone with Mr Pickering, whose undiluted society tended to pall And Lord Wetherby was unhappy because he found Eustace, the monkey, a perpetual strain upon his artistic nerves. It was Eustace who had driven him to his shack in the woods. He could have painted far more comfortably in the house, but Eustace had developed a habit of stealing up to him and plucking the leg of his trousers; and an artist simply cannot give of his best with that sort of thing going on.

Lady Wetherby wrote on. She was not fond of letter-writing and she had allowed her correspondence to accumulate; but she was disposing of it in an energetic and conscientious way, when the entrance of Wrench, the butler, interrupted her.

Wrench had been imported from England at the request of Lord Wetherby, who had said that it soothed him and kept him from feeling home-sick to see a butler about the place. Since then he had been hanging to the establishment as it were by a hair. He gave the impression of being always on the point of giving notice. There were so many things connected with his position of which he disapproved. He had made no official pronouncement of the matter, but Lady Wetherby knew that he disapproved of her classical dancing. His last position had been with the Dowager Duchess of Waveney, the well-known political hostess, who – even had the somewhat generous lines on which she was built not prevented the possibility of such a thing – would have perished rather than dance barefooted in a public restaurant. Wrench also disapproved of America. That fact had been made plain immediately upon his arrival in the country. He had given America one look, and then his mind was made up – he disapproved of it.

'If you please, m'lady!'

Lady Wetherby turned. The butler was looking even more than usually disapproving, and his disapproval had, so to speak, crystallized, as if it had found some more concrete and definite objective than either barefoot dancing or the United States.

'If you please, m'lady – the hape!'

It was Wrench's custom to speak of Eustace in a tone of restrained disgust. He disapproved of Eustace. The Dowager Duchess of Waveney, though she kept open house for members of Parliament, would have drawn the line at monkeys.

'The hape is behaving very strange, m'lady,' said Wrench, frostily.

It has been well said that in this world there is always something. A moment before, Lady Wetherby had been feeling completely contented, without a care on her horizon. It was foolish of her to have expected such a state of things to last, for what is life but a series of sharp corners, round each of which Fate lies in wait for us with a stuffed eel-skin? Something in the butler's manner, a sort of gloating gloom which he radiated, told her that she had arrived at one of these corners now.

'The hape is seated on the kitchen-sink, m'lady, throwing new-laid eggs at the scullery-maid, and cook desired me to step up and ask for instructions.'

'What!' Lady Wetherby rose in agitation. 'What's he doing that for?' she asked, weakly.

A slight, dignified gesture was Wrench's only reply. It was not his place to analyse the motives of monkeys.

'Throwing eggs!'

The sight of Lady Wetherby's distress melted the butler's stern reserve. He unbent so far as to supply a clue.

'As I understand from cook, m'lady, the animal appears to have taken umbrage at a lack of cordiality on the part of the cat. It seems that the hape attempted to fondle the cat, but the latter scratched him; being suspicious,' said Wrench, 'of his *bona fides*.' He scrutinized the ceiling with a dull eye. 'Whereupon,' he continued, 'he seized her tail and threw her with considerable force. He then removed himself to the sink and began to hurl eggs at the scullery-maid.'

Lady Wetherby's mental eye attempted to produce a picture of the scene, but failed.

'I suppose I had better go down and see about it,' she said. Wrench withdrew his gaze from the ceiling.

'I think it would be advisable, m'lady. The scullery-maid is already in hysterics.'

Lady Wetherby led the way to the kitchen. She was wroth with Eustace. This was just the sort of thing out of which Algie would be able to make unlimited capital. It weakened her position with Algie. There was only one thing to do – she must hush it up.

Her first glance, however, at the actual theatre of war gave her the impression that matters had advanced beyond the hushing-up stage. A yellow desolation brooded over the kitchen. It was not so much a kitchen as an omelette. There were eggs everywhere, from floor to ceiling. She crunched her way in on a carpet of oozing shells.

Her entry was a signal for a renewal on a more impressive scale of the uproar that she had heard while opening the door. The air was full of voices. The cook was expressing herself in Norwegian, the parlour-maid in what appeared to be Erse. On a chair in a corner the scullery-maid sobbed and whooped. The odd-job man, who was a baseball enthusiast, was speaking in terms of high praise of Eustace's combined speed and control.

The only calm occupant of the room was Eustace himself, who, either through a shortage of ammunition or through weariness of the pitching-arm, had suspended active hostilities, and was now looking down on the scene from a high shelf. There was a brooding expression in his deep-set eyes. He massaged his right ear with the sole of his left foot in a somewhat *distrait* manner.

'Eustace!' cried Lady Wetherby, severely.

Eustace lowered his foot and gazed at her meditatively, then at the odd-job man, then at the scullery-maid, whose voice rose high above the din.

'I rather fancy, m'lady,' said Wrench, dispassionately, 'that the animal is about to hurl a plate.'

It had escaped the notice of those present that the shelf on which the rioter had taken refuge was within comfortable reach of the dresser, but Eustace himself had not overlooked this important strategic point. As the butler spoke, Eustace picked up a plate and threw it at the scullery-maid, whom he seemed definitely to have picked out as the most hostile of the allies. It was a fast inshoot, and hit the wall just above her head.

''At-a-boy!' said the odd-job man, reverently.

Lady Wetherby turned on him with some violence. His detached attitude was the most irritating of the many irritating aspects of the situation. She paid this man a weekly wage to do odd jobs. The capture of Eustace was essentially an odd job. Yet, instead of doing it, he hung about with the air of one who has paid his half-dollar and bought his bag of peanuts and has now nothing to do but look on and enjoy himself

'Why don't you catch him?' she cried.

The odd-job man came out of his trance. A sudden realization came upon him that life was real and life was earnest, and that if he did not wish to jeopardize a good situation he must bestir himself. Everybody was looking at him expectantly. It seemed to be definitely up to him. It was imperative that, whatever he did, he should do it quickly. There was an apron hanging over the back of a chair. More with the idea of doing something than because he thought he would achieve anything definite thereby, he picked up the apron and flung it at Eustace. Luck was with him. The apron enveloped Eustace just as he was winding up for another inshoot and was off his balance. He tripped and fell, clutched at the apron to save himself, and came to the ground swathed in it, giving the effect of an apron mysteriously endowed with life. The triumphant odd-job man, pressing his advantage like a good general, gathered up the ends, converted it into a rude bag, and one more was added to the long list of the victories of the human over the brute intelligence.

Everybody had a suggestion now. The cook advocated drowning. The parlour-maid favoured the idea of hitting the prisoner with a broom-handle. Wrench, eyeing the struggling apron disapprovingly, mentioned that Mr Pickering had bought a revolver that morning.

'Put him in the coal-cellar,' said Lady Wetherby.

Wrench was more far-seeing.

'If I might offer the warning, m'lady,' said Wrench, 'not the cellar. It is full of coal. It would be placing temptation in the animal's way.'

The odd-job man endorsed this.

'Put him in the garage, then,' said Lady Wetherby.

The odd-job man departed, bearing his heaving bag at arm's length. The cook and the parlour-maid addressed themselves to comforting and healing the scullery-maid. Wrench went off to polish silver, Lady Wetherby to resume her letters. The cat was the last of the party to return to the normal. She came down from the chimney an hour later covered with soot, demanding restoratives.

Lady Wetherby finished her letters. She cut them short, for Eustace's insurgence had interfered with her flow of ideas. She went into the drawing-room, where she found Roscoe Sherriff strumming on the piano.

'Eustace has been raising Cain,' she said.

The Press-agent looked up hopefully. He had been wearing a rather preoccupied air.

'How's that?' he asked.

'Throwing eggs and plates in the kitchen.'

The gleam of interest which had come into Roscoe Sherriff's face died out.

'You couldn't get more than a fill-in at the bottom of a column on that,' he said, regretfully. 'I'm a little disappointed in that monk. I hoped he would pan out bigger. Well, I guess we've just got to give him time. I have an idea that he'll set the house on fire or do something with a punch like that one of these days. You mustn't get discouraged. Why, that puma I made Valerie Devenish keep looked like a perfect failure for four whole months. A child could have played with it. Miss Devenish called me up on the phone, I remember, and said she was darned if she was going to spend the rest of her life maintaining an animal that might as well be stuffed for all the liveliness it showed, and that she was going right out to buy a white mouse instead. Fortunately, I talked her round.

'A few weeks later she came round and thanked me with tears in her eyes. The puma had suddenly struck real mid-season form. It clawed the elevator-boy, bit a postman, held up the traffic for miles, and was finally shot by a policeman. Why, for the next few days there was nothing in the papers at all but Miss Devenish and her puma. There was a war on at the time in Mexico or somewhere, and we had it backed off the front page so far that it was over before it could get back. So, you see, there's always hope. I've been nursing the papers with bits about Eustace, so as to be ready for the grand-stand play when it comes – and all we can do is to wait. It's something if he's been throwing eggs. It shows he's waking up.'

The door opened and Lord Wetherby entered. He looked fatigued. He sank into a chair and sighed.

'I cannot get it,' he said. 'It eludes me.'

He lapsed into a sombre silence.

'What can't you get?' said Lady Wetherby, cautiously.

'The expression – the expression I want to get into the child's eyes in my picture, "Innocence".'

'But you have got it.'

Lord Wetherby shook his head.

'Well, you had when I saw the picture,' persisted Lady Wetherby. 'This child you're painting has just joined the Black Hand. He has been rushed in young over the heads of the waiting list because his father had a pull. Naturally the kid wants to do something to justify his election, and he wants to do it quick. You have caught him at the moment when he sees an old gentleman coming down the street and realizes that he has only got to sneak up and stick his little knife – '

'My dear Polly, I welcome criticism, but this is more – '

Lady Wetherby stroked his coat-sleeve fondly.

'Never mind, Algie, I was only joking, precious. I thought the picture was coming along fine when you showed it to me. I'll come and take another look at it.'

Lord Wetherby shook his head.

'I should have a model. An artist cannot mirror Nature properly without a model. I wish you would invite that child down here.'

'No, Algie, there are limits. I wouldn't have him within a mile of the place.'

'Yet you keep Eustace.'

'Well, you made me engage Wrench. It's fifty-fifty. I wish you wouldn't keep picking on Eustace, Algie dear. He does no harm. Mr Sherriff and I were just saying how peaceable he is. He wouldn't hurt – '

Claire came in.

'Polly,' she said, 'did you put that monkey of yours in the garage? He's just bitten Dudley in the leg.'

Lord Wetherby uttered an exclamation.

'Now perhaps – '

'We went in just now to have a look at the car,' continued Claire. 'Dudley wanted to show me the commutator on the exhaust-box or the windscreen, or something, and he was just bending over when Eustace jumped out from nowhere and pinned him. I'm afraid he has taken it to heart rather.'

Roscoe Sherriff pondered.

'Is this worth half a column?' He shook his head. 'No, I'm afraid not. The public doesn't know Pickering. If it had been Charlie Chaplin or William J. Bryan, or someone on those lines, we could have had the papers bringing out extras. You can visualize William J. Bryan being bitten in the leg by a monkey. It hits you. But Pickering! Eustace might just as well have bitten the leg of the table!'

Lord Wetherby reasserted himself.

'Now that the animal has become a public menace – '

'He's nothing of the kind,' said Lady Wetherby. 'He's only a little upset to-day.'

'Do you mean, Pauline, that even after this you will not get rid of him?'

'Certainly not – poor dear!'

'Very well,' said Lord Wetherby, calmly. 'I give you warning that if he attacks me I shall defend myself.'

He brooded. Lady Wetherby turned to Claire.

'What happened then? Did you shut the door of the garage?'

'Yes, but not until Eustace had got away. He slipped out like a streak and disappeared. It was too dark to see which way he went.'

Dudley Pickering limped heavily into the room.

'I was just telling them about you and Eustace, Dudley.'

Mr Pickering nodded moodily. He was too full for words.

'I think Eustace must be mad,' said Claire.

Roscoe Sherriff uttered a cry of rapture.

'You've said it!' he exclaimed. 'I knew we should get action sooner or later. It's the puma over again. Now we are all right. Now I have something to work on. "Monkey Menaces Country-side." "Long Island Summer Colony in Panic." "Mad Monkey Bites One – "'

A convulsive shudder galvanized Mr Pickering's portly frame.

'"Mad Monkey Terrorizes Long Island. One Dead!"' murmured Roscoe Sherriff, wistfully. 'Do you feel a sort of shooting,

Pickering – a kind of burning sensation under the skin? Lady Wetherby, I guess I'll be getting some of the papers on the phone. We've got a big story.'

He hurried to the telephone, but it was some little time before he could use it. Dudley Pickering was in possession, talking earnestly to the local doctor.

14

It was Nutty Boyd's habit to retire immediately after dinner to his bedroom. What he did there Elizabeth did not know. Sometimes she pictured him reading, sometimes thinking. Neither supposition was correct. Nutty never read. Newspapers bored him and books made his head ache. And as for thinking, he had the wrong shape of forehead. The nearest he ever got to meditation was a sort of trance-like state, a kind of suspended animation in which his mind drifted sluggishly like a log in a backwater. Nutty, it is regrettable to say, went to his room after dinner for the purpose of imbibing two or three surreptitious whiskies-and-sodas.

He behaved in this way, he told himself, purely in order to spare Elizabeth anxiety. There had been in the past a fool of a doctor who had prescribed total abstinence for Nutty, and Elizabeth knew this. Therefore, Nutty held, to take the mildest of drinks with her knowledge would have been to fill her with fears for his safety. So he went to considerable inconvenience to keep the matter from her notice, and thought rather highly of himself for doing so.

It certainly was inconvenient – there was no doubt of that. It made him feel like a cross between a hunted fawn and a burglar. But he had to some extent diminished the possibility of surprise by leaving his door open; and to-night he approached the cupboard where he kept the materials for refreshment with a certain confidence. He had left Elizabeth on the porch in a hammock, apparently anchored for some time. Lord Dawlish was out in the grounds somewhere. Presently he would come in and join Elizabeth on the porch. The risk of interruption was negligible.

Nutty mixed himself a drink and settled down to brood bitterly, as he often did, on the doctor who had made that disastrous statement. Doctors were always saying things like that – sweeping things which nervous people took too literally. It was true that he had been in pretty bad shape at the moment when the words had been spoken. It was just at the end of his Broadway career, when, as he handsomely admitted, there was a certain amount of truth in the opinion that his interior needed a vacation. But since then he had been living in the country, breathing good air, taking things easy. In these altered conditions and after this lapse of time it was absurd to imagine that a moderate amount of alcohol could do him any harm.

It hadn't done him any harm, that was the point. He had tested the doctor's statement and found it incorrect. He had spent three hectic days and nights in New York, and – after a reasonable interval – had felt much the same as usual. And since then he had imbibed each night, and nothing had happened. What it came to was that the doctor was a chump and a blighter. Simply that and nothing more.

Having come to this decision, Nutty mixed another drink. He went to the head of the stairs and listened. He heard nothing. He returned to his room.

Yes, that was it, the doctor was a chump. So far from doing him any harm, these nightly potations brightened Nutty up, gave him heart, and enabled him to endure life in this hole of a place. He felt a certain scornful amusement. Doctors, he supposed, had to get off that sort of talk to earn their money.

He reached out for the bottle, and as he grasped it his eye was caught by something on the floor. A brown monkey with a long, grey tail was sitting there staring at him.

There was one of those painful pauses. Nutty looked at the monkey rather like an elongated Macbeth inspecting the ghost of Banquo. The monkey looked at Nutty. The pause continued. Nutty shut his eyes, counted ten slowly, and opened them. The monkey was still there.

'Boo!' said Nutty, in an apprehensive undertone.

The monkey looked at him.

Nutty shut his eyes again. He would count sixty this time. A cold fear had laid its clammy fingers on his heart. This was what that doctor – not such a chump after all – must have meant!

Nutty began to count. There seemed to be a heavy lump inside him, and his mouth was dry; but otherwise he felt all right. That was the gruesome part of it – this dreadful thing had come upon him at a moment when he could have sworn that he was sound as a bell. If this had happened in the days when he ranged the Great White Way, sucking up deleterious moisture like a cloud, it would have been intelligible. But it had sneaked upon him like a thief in the night; it had stolen unheralded into his life when he had practically reformed. What was the good of practically reforming if this sort of thing was going to happen to one?

'. . . Fifty-nine . . . sixty.'

He opened his eyes. The monkey was still there, in precisely the same attitude, as if it was sitting for its portrait. Panic surged upon Nutty. He lost his head completely. He uttered a wild yell and threw the bottle at the apparition.

Life had not been treating Eustace well that evening. He seemed to have happened upon one of those days when everything goes wrong. The cat had scratched him, the odd-job man had swathed him in an apron, and now this stranger, in whom he had found at first a pleasant restfulness, soothing after the recent scenes of violence in which he had participated, did this to him. He dodged the missile and clambered on to the top of the wardrobe. It was his instinct in times of stress to seek the high spots. And then Elizabeth hurried into the room.

Elizabeth had been lying in the hammock on the porch when her brother's yell had broken forth. It was a lovely, calm, moonlight night, and she had been revelling in the peace of it, when suddenly this outcry from above had shot her out of her hammock like an explosion. She ran upstairs, fearing she knew not what. She found Nutty sitting on the bed, looking like an overwrought giraffe.

'Whatever is the –?' she began; and then things began to impress themselves on her senses.

The bottle which Nutty had thrown at Eustace had missed the latter, but it had hit the wall, and was now lying in many pieces on the floor, and the air was heavy with the scent of it. The remains seemed to leer at her with a kind of furtive swagger, after the manner of broken bottles. A quick thrill of anger ran through Elizabeth. She had always felt more like a mother to Nutty than a sister, and now she would have liked to exercise the maternal privilege of slapping him.

'Nutty!'

'I saw a monkey!' said her brother, hollowly. 'I was standing over there and I saw a monkey! Of course, it wasn't there really. I flung the bottle at it, and it seemed to climb on to that wardrobe.'

'This wardrobe?'

'Yes.'

Elizabeth struck it a resounding blow with the palm of her hand, and Eustace's face popped over the edge, peering down anxiously. 'I can see it now,' said Nutty. A sudden, faint hope came to him. 'Can you see it?' he asked.

Elizabeth did not speak for a moment. This was an unusual situation, and she was wondering how to treat it. She was sorry for Nutty, but Providence had sent this thing and it would be foolish to reject it. She must look on herself in the light of a doctor. It would be kinder to Nutty in the end. She had the feminine aversion from the lie deliberate. Her ethics on the *suggestio falsi* were weak. She looked at Nutty questioningly.

'See it?' she said.

'Don't you see a monkey on the top of the wardrobe?' said Nutty, becoming more definite.

'There's a sort of bit of wood sticking out – '

Nutty sighed.

'No, not that. You didn't see it. I don't think you would.'

He spoke so dejectedly that for a moment Elizabeth weakened, but only for an instant.

'Tell me all about this, Nutty,' she said.

Nutty was beyond the desire for evasion and concealment. His one wish was to tell. He told all.

'But, Nutty, how silly of you!'

'Yes.'

'After what the doctor said.'

'I know.'

'You remember his telling you –'

'I know. Never again!'

'What do you mean?'

'I quit. I'm going to give it up.'

Elizabeth embraced him maternally.

'That's a good child!' she said. 'You really promise?'

'I don't have to promise, I'm just going to do it.'

Elizabeth compromised with her conscience by becoming soothing.

'You know, this isn't so very serious, Nutty, darling. I mean, it's just a warning.'

'It's warned me all right.'

'You will be perfectly all right if –'

Nutty interrupted her.

'You're sure you can't see anything?'

'See what?'

Nutty's voice became almost apologetic.

'I know it's just imagination, but the monkey seems to me to be climbing down from the wardrobe.'

'I can't see anything climbing down the wardrobe,' said Elizabeth, as Eustace touched the floor.

'It's come down now. It's crossing the carpet.'

'Where?'

'It's gone now. It went out of the door.'

'Oh!'

'I say, Elizabeth, what do you think I ought to do?'

'I should go to bed and have a nice long sleep, and you'll feel –'

'Somehow I don't feel much like going to bed. This sort of thing upsets a chap, you know.'

'Poor dear!'

'I think I'll go for a long walk.'

'That's a splendid idea.'

'I think I'd better do a good lot of walking from now on. Didn't Chalmers bring down some Indian clubs with him? I think I'll borrow them. I ought to keep out in the open a lot, I think. I wonder if there's any special diet I ought to have. Well, anyway, I'll be going for that walk.'

At the foot of the stairs Nutty stopped. He looked quickly into the porch, then looked away again.

'What's the matter?' asked Elizabeth.

'I thought for a moment I saw the monkey sitting on the hammock.'

He went out of the house and disappeared from view down the drive, walking with long, rapid strides.

Elizabeth's first act, when he had gone, was to fetch a banana from the ice-box. Her knowledge of monkeys was slight, but she fancied they looked with favour on bananas. It was her intention to conciliate Eustace.

She had placed Eustace by now. Unlike Nutty, she read the papers, and she knew all about Lady Wetherby and her pets. The fact that Lady Wetherby, as she had been informed by the grocer in friendly talk, had rented a summer house in the neighbourhood made Eustace's identity positive.

She had no very clear plans as to what she intended to do with Eustace, beyond being quite resolved that she was going to board and lodge him for a few days. Nutty had had the jolt he needed, but it might be that the first freshness of it would wear away, in which event it would be convenient to have Eustace on the premises. She regarded Eustace as a sort of medicine. A second dose might not be necessary, but it was as well to have the mixture handy. She took another banana, in case the first might not be sufficient. She then returned to the porch.

Eustace was sitting on the hammock, brooding. The complexities of life were weighing him down a good deal. He was not aware of Elizabeth's presence until he found her standing by him. He had just braced himself for flight, when he perceived that she bore rich gifts.

Eustace was always ready for a light snack – readier now

than usual, for air and exercise had sharpened his appetite. He took the banana in a detached manner, as if to convey the idea that it did not commit him to any particular course of conduct. It was a good banana, and he stretched out a hand for the other. Elizabeth sat down beside him, but he did not move. He was convinced now of her good intentions. It was thus that Lord Dawlish found them when he came in from the garden.

'Where has your brother gone to?' he asked. 'He passed me just now at eight miles an hour. Great Scot! What's that?'

'It's a monkey. Don't frighten him; he's rather nervous.'

She tickled Eustace under the ear, for their relations were now friendly.

'Nutty went for a walk because he thought he saw it.'

'Thought he saw it?'

'Thought he saw it,' repeated Elizabeth, firmly. 'Will you remember, Mr Chalmers, that, as far as he is concerned, this monkey has no existence?'

'I don't understand.'

Elizabeth explained.

'You see now?'

'I see. But how long are you going to keep the animal?'

'Just a day or two – in case.'

'Where are you going to keep it?'

'In the outhouse. Nutty never goes there, it's too near the bee-hives.'

'I suppose you don't know who the owner is?'

'Yes, I do; it must be Lady Wetherby.'

'Lady Wetherby!'

'She's a woman who dances at one of the restaurants. I read in a Sunday paper about her monkey. She has just taken a house near here. I don't see who else the animal could belong to. Monkeys are rarities on Long Island.'

Bill was silent. 'Sudden a thought came like a full-blown rose, flushing his brow.' For days he had been trying to find an excuse for calling on Lady Wetherby as a first step toward meeting Claire again. Here it was. There would be no need to interfere with Elizabeth's plans. He would be vague. He would say he had just seen the runaway, but would not add where. He would create an atmosphere of helpful sympathy. Perhaps, later on, Elizabeth would let him take the monkey back.

'What are you thinking about?' asked Elizabeth.

'Oh, nothing,' said Bill.

'Perhaps we had better stow away our visitor for the night.'

'Yes.'

Elizabeth got up.

'Poor, dear Nutty may be coming back at any moment now,' she said.

But poor, dear Nutty did not return for a full two hours. When he did he was dusty and tired, but almost cheerful.

'I didn't see the brute once all the time I was out,' he told Elizabeth. 'Not once!'

Elizabeth kissed him fondly and offered to heat water for a bath; but Nutty said he would take it cold. From now on, he vowed, nothing but cold baths. He conveyed the impression of being a blend of repentant sinner and hardy Norseman. Before he went to bed he approached Bill on the subject of Indian clubs.

'I want to get myself into shape, old top,' he said.

'Yes?'

'I've got to cut it out – to-night I thought I saw a monkey.'

'Really?'

'As plain as I see you now.' Nutty gave the clubs a tentative swing. 'What do you do with these darned things? Swing them about and all that? All right, I see the idea. Good night.'

But Bill did not pass a good night. He lay awake long, thinking over his plans for the morrow.

15

LADY WETHERBY was feeling battered. She had not realized how seriously Roscoe Sherriff took the art of publicity, nor what would be the result of the half-hour he had spent at the telephone on the night of the departure of Eustace.

Roscoe Sherriff's eloquence had fired the imagination of editors. There had been a notable lack of interesting happenings this summer. Nobody seemed to be striking or murdering or having violent accidents. The universe was torpid. In these circumstances, the escape of Eustace seemed to present possibilities. Reporters had been sent down. There were three of them living in the house now, and Wrench's air of disapproval was deepening every hour.

It was their strenuousness which had given Lady Wetherby that battered feeling. There was strenuousness in the air, and she resented it on her vacation. She had come to Long Island to vegetate, and with all this going on round her vegetation was impossible. She was not long alone. Wrench entered.

'A gentleman to see you, m'lady.'

In the good old days, when she had been plain Polly Davis, of the personnel of the chorus of various musical comedies, Lady Wetherby would have suggested a short way of disposing of this untimely visitor; but she had a position to keep up now.

'From some darned paper?' she asked, wearily.

'No, m'lady. I fancy he is not connected with the Press.'

There was something in Wrench's manner that perplexed Lady Wetherby, something almost human, as if Wrench were on the point of coming alive. She did not guess it, but the explanation was that Bill, quite unwittingly, had impressed Wrench. There was that about Bill that reminded the butler of London and dignified receptions at the house of the Dowager Duchess of Waveney. It was deep calling unto deep.

'Where is he?'

'I have shown him into the drawing-room, m'lady.'

Lady Wetherby went downstairs and found a large young man awaiting her, looking nervous.

Bill was feeling nervous. A sense of the ridiculousness of his mission had come upon him. After all, he asked himself, what on earth had he got to say? A presentiment had come upon him that he was about to look a perfect ass. At the sight of Lady Wetherby his nervousness began to diminish. Lady Wetherby was not a formidable person. In spite of her momentary peevishness, she brought with her an atmosphere of geniality and camaraderie.

'It's about your monkey,' he said, coming to the point at once.

Lady Wetherby brightened.

'Oh! Have you seen it?'

He was glad that she put it like that.

'Yes. It came round our way last night.'

'Where is that?'

'I am staying at a farm near here, a place they call Flack's. The monkey got into one of the rooms.'

'Yes?'

'And then – er – then it got out again, don't you know.'

Lady Wetherby looked disappointed.

'So it may be anywhere now?' she said.

In the interests of truth, Bill thought it best to leave this question unanswered.

'Well, it's very good of you to have bothered to come out and tell me,' said Lady Wetherby. 'It gives us a clue, at any rate. Thank you. At least, we know now in which direction it went.'

There was a pause. Bill gathered that the other was looking on the interview as terminated, and that she was expecting him to go, and he had not begun to say what he wanted to say. He tried to think of a way of introducing the subject of Claire that should not seem too abrupt.

'Er –' he said.

'Well?' said Lady Wetherby, simultaneously.

'I beg your pardon.'

'You have the floor,' said Lady Wetherby. 'Shoot!'

It was not what she had intended to say. For months she had been trying to get out of the habit of saying that sort of thing, but she still suffered relapses. Only the other day she had told Wrench to check some domestic problem or other with his hat, and he had nearly given notice. But if she had been intending to put Bill at his ease she could not have said anything better.

'You have a Miss Fenwick staying with you, haven't you?' he said.

Lady Wetherby beamed.

'Do you know Claire?'

'Yes, rather!'

'She's my best friend. We used to be in the same company when I was in England.'

'So she has told me.'

'She was my bridesmaid when I married Lord Wetherby.'

'Yes.'

Lady Wetherby was feeling perfectly happy now, and when Lady Wetherby felt happy she always became garrulous. She was one of those people who are incapable of looking on anybody as a stranger after five minutes' acquaintance. Already she had begun to regard Bill as an old friend.

'Those were great days,' she said, cheerfully. 'None of us had a bean, and Algie was the hardest up of the whole bunch. After we were married we went to the Savoy for the wedding-breakfast, and when it was over and the waiter came with the check, Algie said he was sorry, but he had had a bad week at Lincoln and hadn't the price on him. He tried to touch me, but I passed. Then he had a go at the best man, but the best man had nothing in the world but one suit of clothes and a spare collar. Claire was broke, too, so the end of it was that the best man had to sneak out and pawn my watch and the wedding-ring.'

The room rang with her reminiscent laughter, Bill supplying a bass accompaniment. Bill was delighted. He had never hoped that it would be granted to him to become so rapidly intimate with Claire's hostess. Why, he had only to keep the conversation in this chummy vein for a little while longer and she would give him the run of the house.

'Miss Fenwick isn't in now, I suppose?' he asked.

'No, Claire's out with Dudley Pickering. You don't know him, do you?'

'No.'

'She's engaged to him.'

It is an ironical fact that Lady Wetherby was by nature one of the firmest believers in existence in the policy of breaking things gently to people. She had a big, soft heart, and she hated hurting her fellows. As a rule, when she had bad news to impart to any one she administered the blow so gradually and with such mystery as to the actual facts that the victim, having passed through the various stages of imagined horrors, was genuinely relieved, when she actually came to the point, to find that all that had happened was that he had lost all his money. But now in perfect innocence, thinking only to pass along an interesting bit of information, she had crushed Bill as effectively as if she had used a club for that purpose.

'I'm tickled to death about it,' she went on, as it were over her hearer's prostrate body. It was I who brought them together, you know. I wrote telling Claire to come out here on the *Atlantic,* knowing that Dudley was sailing on that boat. I had an idea they would hit it off together. Dudley fell for her right away, and she must have fallen for him, for they had only known each other for a few weeks when they came and told me they were engaged. It happened last Sunday.'

'Last Sunday!'

It had seemed to Bill a moment before that he would never again be capable of speech, but this statement dragged the words out of him. Last Sunday! Why, it was last Sunday that Claire had broken off her engagement with him!

'Last Sunday at nine o'clock in the evening, with a full moon shining and soft music going on off-stage. Real third-act stuff.'

Bill felt positively dizzy. He groped back in his memory for facts. He had gone out for his walk after dinner. They had dined at eight. He had been walking some time. Why, in Heaven's name, this was the quickest thing in the amatory annals of civilization! His brain was too numbed to work out a perfectly accurate schedule, but it looked as if she must have got engaged to this Pickering person before she met him, Bill, in the road that night.

'It's a wonderful match for dear old Claire,' resumed Lady Wetherby, twisting the knife in the wound with a happy unconsciousness. 'Dudley's not only a corking good fellow, but he has thirty million dollars stuffed away in the stocking and a business that brings him in a perfectly awful mess of money every year. He's the Pickering of the Pickering automobiles, you know.'

Bill got up. He stood for a moment holding to the back of his chair before speaking. It was almost exactly thus that he had felt in the days when he had gone in for boxing and had stopped forceful swings with the more sensitive portions of his person.

'That – that's splendid!' he said. 'I – I think I'll be going.'

'I heard the car outside just now,' said Lady Wetherby. 'I think it's probably Claire and Dudley come back. Won't you wait and see her?'

Bill shook his head.

'Well, good-bye for the present, then. You must come round again. Any friend of Claire's – and it was bully of you to bother about looking in to tell of Eustace.'

Bill had reached the door. He was about to turn the handle when someone turned it on the other side.

'Why, here is Dudley,' said Lady Wetherby. 'Dudley, this is a friend of Claire's.'

Dudley Pickering was one of those men who take the ceremony of introduction with a measured solemnity. It was his practice to grasp the party of the second part firmly by the hand, hold it, look into his eyes in a reverent manner, and get off some little speech of appreciation, short but full of feeling. The opening part of this ceremony he performed now. He grasped Bill's hand firmly, held it, and looked into his eyes. And then, having performed his business, he fell down on his lines. Not a word proceeded from him. He dropped the hand and stared at Bill amazedly and – more than that – with fear.

Bill, too, uttered no word. It was not one of those chatty meetings.

But if they were short on words, both Bill and Mr Pickering were long on looks. Bill stared at Mr Pickering. Mr Pickering stared at Bill.

Bill was drinking in Mr Pickering. The stoutness of Mr Pickering – the elderliness of Mr Pickering – the dullness of Mr Pickering – all these things he perceived. And illumination broke upon him.

Mr Pickering was drinking in Bill. The largeness of Bill – the embarrassment of Bill – the obvious villainy of Bill – none of these things escaped his notice. And illumination broke upon him also.

For Dudley Pickering, in the first moment of their meeting, had recognized Bill as the man who had been lurking in the grounds and peering in at the window, the man at whom on the night when he had become engaged to Claire he had shouted 'Hi!'

'Where's Claire, Dudley?' asked Lady Wetherby.

Mr Pickering withdrew his gaze reluctantly from Bill.

'Gone upstairs.'

'I'll go and tell her that you're here, Mr – You never told me your name.'

Bill came to life with an almost acrobatic abruptness. There were many things of which at that moment he felt absolutely incapable, and meeting Claire was one of them.

'No; I must be going,' he said, hurriedly. 'Good-bye.'

He came very near running out of the room. Lady Wetherby regarded the practically slammed door with wide eyes.

'Quick exit of Nut Comedian!' she said. 'Whatever was the matter with the man? He's scorched a trail in the carpet.'

Mr Pickering was trembling violently.

'Do you know who that was? He was the man!' said Mr Pickering.

'What man?'

'The man I caught looking in at the window that night!'

'What nonsense! You must be mistaken. He said he knew Claire quite well.'

'But when you suggested that he should meet her he ran.'

This aspect of the matter had not occurred to Lady Wetherby.

'So he did!'

'What did he tell you that showed he knew Claire?'

'Well, now that I come to think of it, he didn't tell me anything. I did the talking. He just sat there.'

Mr Pickering quivered with combined fear and excitement and inductive reasoning.

'It was a trick!' he cried. 'Remember what Sherriff said that night when I told you about finding the man looking in at the window? He said that the fellow was spying round as a preliminary move. To-day he trumps up an obviously false excuse for getting into the house. Was he left alone in the rooms at all?'

'Yes. Wrench loosed him in here and then came up to tell me.'

'For several minutes, then, he was alone in the house. Why, he had time to do all he wanted to do!'

'Calm down!'

'I am perfectly calm. But –'

'You've been seeing too many crook plays, Dudley. A man isn't necessarily a burglar because he wears a decent suit of clothes.'

'Why was he lurking in the grounds that night?'

'You're just imagining that it was the same man.'

'I am absolutely positive it was the same man.'

'Well, we can easily settle one thing about him, at any rate. Here comes Claire. Claire, old girl,' she said, as the door opened, 'do you know a man named – Darn it! I never got his name, but he's –'

Claire stood in the doorway, looking from one to the other.

'What's the matter, Dudley?' she said.

'Dudley's gone clean up in the air,' explained Lady Wetherby, tolerantly. 'A friend of yours called to tell me he had seen Eustace –'

'So that was his excuse, was it?' said Dudley Pickering. 'Did he say where Eustace was?'

'No; he said he had seen him; that was all '

'An obviously trumped-up story. He had heard of Eustace's escape and he knew that any story connected with him would be a passport into the house.'

Lady Wetherby turned to Claire.

'You haven't told us yet if you know the man. He was a big, tall, broad gazook,' said Lady Wetherby. 'Very English '

'He faked the English,' said Dudley Pickering. 'That man was no more an Englishman than I am.'

'Be patient with him, Claire,' urged Lady Wetherby. 'He's been going to the movies too much, and thinks every man who has had his trousers pressed is a social gangster. This man was the most English thing I've ever seen – talked like this.'

She gave a passable reproduction of Bill's speech. Claire started.

'I don't know him!' she cried.

Her mind was in a whirl of agitation. Why had Bill come to the house? What had he said? Had he told Dudley anything?

'I don't recognize the description,' she said, quickly. 'I don't know anything about him.'

'There!' said Dudley Pickering, triumphantly.

'It's queer,' said Lady Wetherby. 'You're sure you don't know him, Claire?'

'Absolutely sure.'

'He said he was living at a place near here, called Flack's.'

'I know the place,' said Dudley Pickering. 'A sinister, tumble-down sort of place. Just where a bunch of crooks would be living.'

'I thought it was a bee-farm,' said Lady Wetherby. 'One of the tradesmen told me about it. I saw a most corkingly pretty girl bicycling down to the village one morning, and they told me she was named Boyd and kept a bee-farm at Flack's.'

'A blind!' said Mr Pickering, stoutly. 'The girl's the man's accomplice. It's quite easy to see the way they work. The girl comes and settles in the place so that everybody knows her. That's to lull suspicion. Then the man comes down for a visit and goes about cleaning up the neighbouring houses. You can't get away from the fact that this summer there have been half a dozen burglaries down here, and nobody has found out who did them.'

Lady Wetherby looked at him indulgently.

'And now,' she said, 'having got us scared stiff, what are you going to do about it?'

'I am going,' he said, with determination, 'to take steps.'

He went out quickly, the keen, tense man of affairs.

'Bless him!' said Lady Wetherby. 'I'd no idea your Dudley had so much imagination, Claire. He's a perfect bomb-shell.'

Claire laughed shakily.

'It is odd, though,' said Lady Wetherby, meditatively, 'that this man should have said that he knew you, when you don't –'

Claire turned impulsively.

'Polly, I want to tell you something. Promise you won't tell Dudley. I wasn't telling the truth just now. I do know this man. I was engaged to him once.'

'What!'

'For goodness' sake don't tell Dudley!'

'But –'

'It's all over now; but I used to be engaged to him.'

'Not when I was in England?'

'No, after that.'

'Then he didn't know you are engaged to Dudley now?'

'N-no. I – I haven't seen him for a long time.'

Lady Wetherby looked remorseful.

'Poor man! I must have given him a jolt! But why didn't you tell me about him before?'

'Oh, I don't know.'

'Oh, well, I'm not inquisitive. There's no rubber in my composition. It's your affair.'

'You won't tell Dudley?'

'Of course not. But why not? You've nothing to be ashamed of.'

'No; but –'

'Well, I won't tell him, anyway. But I'm glad you told me about him. Dudley was so eloquent about burglars that he almost had me going. I wonder where he rushed off to?'

Dudley Pickering had rushed off to his bedroom, and was examining a revolver there. He examined it carefully, keenly. Preparedness was Dudley Pickering's slogan. He looked rather like a stout sheriff in a film drama.

16

IN the interesting land of India, where snakes abound and scorpions are common objects of the wayside, a native who has had the misfortune to be bitten by one of the latter pursues an admirably common-sense plan. He does not stop to lament, nor does he hang about analysing his emotions. He runs and runs and runs, and keeps on running until he has worked the poison out of his system. Not until then does he attempt introspection.

Lord Dawlish, though ignorant of this fact, pursued almost identically the same policy. He did not run on leaving Lady Wetherby's house, but he took a very long and very rapid walk, than which in times of stress there are few things of greater medicinal value to the human mind. To increase the similarity, he was conscious of a curious sense of being poisoned. He felt stifled – in want of air.

Bill was a simple young man, and he had a simple code of ethics. Above all things he prized and admired and demanded from his friends the quality of straightness. It was his one demand. He had never actually had a criminal friend, but he was quite capable of intimacy with even a criminal, provided only that there was something spacious about his brand of crime and that it did not involve anything mean or underhand. It was the fact that Mr Breitstein whom Claire had wished him to insinuate into his club, though acquitted of actual crime, had been proved guilty of meanness and treachery, that had so prejudiced Bill against him. The worst accusation that he could bring against a man was that he was not square, that he had not played the game.

Claire had not been square. It was that, more than the shock of surprise of Lady Wetherby's news, that had sent him striding along the State Road at the rate of five miles an hour, staring before him with unseeing eyes. A sudden recollection of their last interview brought a dull flush to Bill's face and accelerated his speed. He felt physically ill.

It was not immediately that he had arrived at even this sketchy outline of his feelings. For perhaps a mile he walked as the scorpion-stung natives run – blindly, wildly, with nothing in his mind but a desire to walk faster and faster, to walk as no man had ever walked before. And then – one does not wish to be unduly realistic, but the fact is too important to be ignored – he began to perspire. And hard upon that unrefined but wonder-working flow came a certain healing of spirit.

Dimly at first, but every moment more clearly, he found it possible to think.

In a man of Bill's temperament there are so many qualities wounded by a blow such as he had received, that it is hardly surprising that his emotions, when he began to examine them, were mixed. Now one, now another, of his wounds presented itself to his notice. And then individual wounds would become difficult to distinguish in the mass of injuries. Spiritually, he was in the position of a man who has been hit simultaneously in a number of sensitive spots by a variety of hard and hurtful things. He was as little able, during the early stages of his meditations, to say where he was hurt most as a man who had been stabbed in the back, bitten in the ankle, hit in the eye, smitten with a blackjack, and kicked on the shin in the same moment of time. All that such a man would be able to say with certainty would be that unpleasant things had happened to him; and that was all that Bill was able to say.

Little by little, walking swiftly the while, he began to make a rough inventory. He sorted out his injuries, catalogued them. It was perhaps his self-esteem that had suffered least of all, for he was by nature modest. He had a savage humility, valuable in a crisis of this sort.

But he looked up to Claire. He had thought her straight. And all the time that she had been saying those things to him that night of their last meeting she had been engaged to another man, a fat, bald, doddering, senile fool, whose only merit was his money. Scarcely a fair description of Mr Pickering, but in a man in Bill's position a little bias is excusable.

Bill walked on. He felt as if he could walk for ever. Automobiles whirred past, hooting peevishly, but he heeded them not. Dogs trotted out to exchange civilities, but he ignored them. The poison in his blood drove him on.

And then quite suddenly and unexpectedly the fever passed. Almost in mid-stride he became another man, a healed, sane man, keenly aware of a very vivid thirst and a desire to sit down and rest before attempting the ten miles of cement road that lay between him and home. Half an hour at a wayside inn completed the cure. It was a weary but clear-headed Bill who trudged back through the gathering dusk.

He found himself thinking of Claire as of someone he had known long ago, someone who had never touched his life. She seemed so far away that he wondered how she could ever have affected him for pain or pleasure. He looked at her across a chasm. This is the real difference between love and infatuation, that infatuation can be slain cleanly with a single blow. In the hour of clear vision which had come to him, Bill saw that he had never loved Claire. It was her beauty that had held him, that and the appeal which her circumstances had made to his pity. Their minds had not run smoothly together. Always there had been something that jarred, a subtle antagonism. And she was crooked.

Almost unconsciously his mind began to build up an image of the ideal girl, the girl he would have liked Claire to be, the girl who would conform to all that he demanded of woman. She would be brave. He realized now that, even though it had moved his pity, Claire's querulousness had offended something in him.

He had made allowances for her, but the ideal girl would have had no need of allowances. The ideal girl would be plucky, cheerfully valiant, a fighter. She would not admit the existence of hard luck.

She would be honest. Here, too, she would have no need of allowances. No temptation would be strong enough to make her do a mean act or think a mean thought, for her courage would give her strength, and her strength would make her proof against temptation. She would be kind. That was because she would also be extremely intelligent, and, being extremely intelligent, would have need of kindness to enable her to bear with a not very intelligent man like himself. For the rest, she would be small and alert and pretty, and fair haired – and brown-eyed – and she would keep a bee farm and her name would be Elizabeth Boyd.

Having arrived with a sense of mild astonishment at this conclusion, Bill found, also to his surprise, that he had walked ten miles without knowing it and that he was turning in at the farm gate. Somebody came down the drive, and he saw that it was Elizabeth.

She hurried to meet him, small and shadowy in the uncertain light. James, the cat, stalked rheumatically at her side. She came up to Bill, and he saw that her face wore an anxious look. He gazed at her with a curious feeling that it was a very long time since he had seen her last.

'Where have you been?' she said, her voice troubled. 'I couldn't think what had become of you.'

'I went for a walk.'

'But you've been gone hours and hours.'

'I went to a place called Morrisville.'

'Morrisville!' Elizabeth's eyes opened wide. 'Have you walked twenty miles?'

'Why, I – I believe I have.'

It was the first time he had been really conscious of it. Elizabeth looked at him in consternation. Perhaps it was the association in her mind of unexpected walks with the newly-born activities of the repentant Nutty that gave her the feeling that there must be some mental upheaval on a large scale at the back of this sudden ebullition of long-distance pedestrianism. She remembered that the thought had come to her once or twice during the past week that all was not well with her visitor, and that he had seemed downcast and out of spirits.

She hesitated.

'Is anything the matter, Mr Chalmers?'

'No,' said Bill, decidedly. He would have found a difficulty in making that answer with any ring of conviction earlier in the day, but now it was different. There was nothing whatever the matter with him now. He had never felt happier.

'You're sure?'

'Absolutely. I feel fine.'

'I thought – I've been thinking for some days – that you might be in trouble of some sort.'

Bill swiftly added another to that list of qualities which he had been framing on his homeward journey. That girl of his would be angelically sympathetic.

'It's awfully good of you,' he said, 'but honestly I feel like – I feel great.'

The little troubled look passed from Elizabeth's face. Her eyes twinkled.

'You're really feeling happy?'

'Tremendously.'

'Then let me damp you. We're in an awful fix!'

'What! In what way?'

'About the monkey.'

'Has he escaped?'

'That's the trouble – he hasn't.'

'I don't understand.'

'Come and sit down and I'll tell you. It's a shame to keep you standing after your walk.'

They made their way to the massive stone seat which Mr Flack, the landlord, had bought at a sale and dumped in a moment of exuberance on the farm grounds.

'This is the most hideous thing on earth,' said Elizabeth casually, 'but it will do to sit on. Now tell me: why did you go to Lady Wetherby's this afternoon?'

It was all so remote, it seemed so long ago that he had wanted to find an excuse for meeting Claire again, that for a moment Bill hesitated in actual perplexity, and before he could speak Elizabeth had answered the question for him.

'I suppose you went out of kindness of heart to relieve the poor lady's mind,' she said. 'But you certainly did the wrong thing. You started something!'

'I didn't tell her the animal was here.'

'What did you tell her?'

'I said I had seen it, don't you know.'

'That was enough.'

'I'm awfully sorry.'

'Oh, we shall pull through all right, but we must act at once. We must be swift and resolute. We must saddle our chargers and up and away, and all that sort of thing. Show a flash of speed,' she explained kindly, at the sight of Bill's bewildered face.

'But what has happened?'

'The press is on our trail. I've been interviewing reporters all the afternoon.'

'Reporters!'

'Millions of them. The place is alive with them. Keen, hatchet-faced young men, and every one of them was the man who really unravelled some murder mystery or other, though the police got the credit for it. They told me so.'

'But, I say, how on earth –'

'– did they get here? I suppose Lady Wetherby invited them.'

'But why?'

'She wants the advertisement, of course. I know it doesn't sound sensational – a lost monkey; but when it's a celebrity's lost monkey it makes a difference. Suppose King George had lost a monkey; wouldn't your London newspapers give it a good deal of space? Especially if it had thrown eggs at one of the ladies and bitten the Duke of Norfolk in the leg? That's what our visitor has been doing apparently. At least, he threw eggs at the scullery-maid and bit a millionaire. It's practically the same thing. At any rate, there it is. The newspaper men are here, and they seem to regard this farm as their centre of operations. I had the greatest difficulty in inducing them to go home to their well-earned dinners. They wanted to camp out on the place. As it is, there may still be some of them round, hiding in the grass with notebooks, and telling one another in whispers that they were the men who really solved the murder mystery. What shall we do?'

Bill had no suggestions.

'You realize our position? I wonder if we could be arrested for kidnapping. The monkey is far more human than most of the millionaire children who get kidnapped. It's an awful fix. Did you know that Lady Wetherby is going to offer a reward for the animal?'

'No, really?'

'Five hundred dollars!'

'Surely not!'

'She is. I suppose she feels she can charge it up to necessary expenses for publicity and still be ahead of the game, taking into account the advertising she's going to get.'

'She said nothing about that when I saw her.'

'No, because it won't be offered until to-morrow or the day after. One of the newspaper men told me that. The idea is, of course, to make the thing exciting just when it would otherwise be dying as a news item. Cumulative interest. It's a good scheme, too, but it makes it very awkward for me. I don't want to be in the position of keeping a monkey locked up with the idea of waiting until somebody starts a bull market in monkeys. I consider that that sort of thing would stain the spotless escutcheon of the Boyds. It would be a low trick for that old-established family to play. Not but what poor, dear Nutty would do it like a shot,' she concluded meditatively.

Bill was impressed.

'It does make it awkward, what?'

'It makes it more than awkward, what! Take another aspect of the situation. The night before last my precious Nutty, while ruining his constitution with the demon rum, thought he saw a monkey that wasn't there, and instantly resolved to lead a new and better life. He hates walking, but he has now begun to do his five miles a day. He loathes cold baths, but he now wallows in them. I don't know his views on Indian clubs, but I should think that he has a strong prejudice against them, too, but now you can't go near him without taking a chance of being brained. Are all these good things to stop as quickly as they began? If I know Nutty, he would drop them exactly one minute after he heard that it was a real monkey he saw that night. And how are we to prevent his hearing? By a merciful miracle he was out taking his walk when the newspaper men began to infest the place to-day, but that might not happen another time. What conclusion does all this suggest to you, Mr Chalmers?'

'We ought to get rid of the animal.'

'This very minute. But don't you bother to come. You must be tired out, poor thing.'

'I never felt less tired,' said Bill stoutly.

Elizabeth looked at him in silence for a moment.

'You're rather splendid, you know, Mr Chalmers. You make

a great partner for an adventure of this kind. You're nice and solid.'

The outhouse lay in the neighbourhood of the hives, a gaunt, wooden structure surrounded by bushes. Elizabeth glanced over her shoulder as she drew the key from her pocket.

'You can't think how nervous I was this afternoon,' she said. 'I thought every moment one of those newspaper men would look in here. I – James! James! I thought I heard James in those bushes – I kept heading them away. Once I thought it was all up.' She unlocked the door. 'One of them was about a yard from the window, just going to look in. Thank goodness, a bee stung him at the psychological moment, and – Oh!'

'What's the matter?'

'Come and get a banana.'

They walked to the house. On the way Elizabeth stopped.

'Why, you haven't had any dinner either!' she said.

'Never mind me,' said Bill, 'I can wait. Let's get this thing finished first.'

'You really are a sport, Mr Chalmers,' said Elizabeth gratefully. 'It would kill me to wait a minute. I shan't feel happy until I've got it over. Will you stay here while I go up and see that Nutty's safe in his room?' she added as they entered the house.

She stopped abruptly. A feline howl had broken the stillness of the night, followed instantly by a sharp report.

'What was that?'

'It sounded like a car backfiring.'

'No, it was a shot. One of the neighbours, I expect. You can hear miles away on a night like this. I suppose a cat was after his chickens. Thank goodness, James isn't a pirate cat. Wait while I go up and see Nutty.'

She was gone only a moment.

'It's all right,' she said. 'I peeped in. He's doing deep breathing exercises at his window which looks out the other way. Come along.'

When they reached the outhouse they found the door open.

'Did you do that?' said Elizabeth. 'Did you leave it open?'

'No.'

'I don't remember doing it myself. It must have swung open. Well, this saves us a walk. He'll have gone.'

'Better take a look round, what?'

'Yes, I suppose so; but he's sure not to be there. Have you a match?'

Bill struck one and held it up.

'Good Lord!'

The match went out.

'What is it? What has happened?'

Bill was fumbling for another match.

'There's something on the floor. It looks like – I thought for a minute –' The small flame shot out of the gloom, flickered, then burned with a steady glow. Bill stooped, bending over something on the ground. The match burned down.

Bill's voice came out of the darkness:

'I say, you were right about that noise. It was a shot. The poor little chap's down there on the floor with a hole in him the size of my fist.'

17

BOYHOOD, like measles, is one of those complaints which a man should catch young and have done with, for when it comes in middle life it is apt to be serious. Dudley Pickering had escaped boyhood at the time when his contemporaries were contracting it. It is true that for a few years after leaving the cradle he had exhibited a certain immatureness, but as soon as he put on knickerbockers and began to go about a little he outgrew all that. He avoided altogether the chaotic period which usually lies between the years of ten and fourteen. At ten he was a thoughtful and sober-minded young man, at fourteen almost an old fogy.

And now – thirty-odd years overdue – boyhood had come upon him. As he examined the revolver in his bedroom, wild and unfamiliar emotions seethed within him. He did not realize it, but they were the emotions which should have come to him thirty years before and driven him out to hunt Indians in the garden. An imagination which might well have become atrophied through disuse had him as thoroughly in its control as ever he had had his Pickering Giant.

He believed almost with devoutness in the plot which he had detected for the spoliation of Lord Wetherby's summer-house, that plot of which he held Lord Dawlish to be the mainspring. And it must be admitted that circumstances had combined to help his belief. If the atmosphere in which he was moving was not sinister then there was no meaning in the word.

Summer homes had been burgled, there was no getting away from that – half a dozen at least in the past two months. He was a stranger in the locality, so had no means of knowing that summer homes were always burgled on Long Island every year, as regularly as the coming of the mosquito and the advent of the jelly-fish. It was one of the local industries. People left summer homes lying about loose in lonely spots, and you just naturally got in through the cellar window. Such was the Long Islander's simple creed.

This created in Mr Pickering's mind an atmosphere of burglary, a receptiveness, as it were, toward burglars as phenomena, and the extremely peculiar behaviour of the person whom in his thoughts he always referred to as The Man crystallized it. He had seen The Man hanging about, peering in at windows. He had shouted 'Hi!' and The Man had run. The Man had got into the house under the pretence of being a friend of Claire's. At the suggestion that he should meet Claire he had dashed away in a panic. And Claire, both then and later, had denied absolutely any knowledge of him.

As for the apparently blameless beekeeping that was going on at the place where he lived, that was easily discounted. Mr Pickering had heard somewhere or read somewhere – he rather thought that it was in those interesting but disturbing chronicles of Raffles – that the first thing an intelligent burglar did was to assume some open and innocent occupation to avert possible inquiry into his real mode of life. Mr Pickering did not put it so to himself, for he was rarely slangy even in thought, but what he felt was that he had caught The Man and his confederate with the goods.

If Mr Pickering had had his boyhood at the proper time and finished with it, he would no doubt have acted otherwise than he did. He would have contented himself with conducting a war of defence. He would have notified the police, and considered that all that remained for him personally to do was to stay in his room at night with his revolver. But boys will be boys. The only course that seemed to him in any way satisfactory in this his hour of rejuvenation was to visit the bee farm, the hotbed of crime, and keep an eye on it. He wanted to go there and prowl.

He did not anticipate any definite outcome of his visit. In his boyish, elemental way he just wanted to take a revolver and a pocketful of cartridges, and prowl.

It was a great night for prowling. A moon so little less than full that the eye could barely detect its slight tendency to become concave, shone serenely, creating a desirable combination of black shadows where the prowler might hide and great stretches of light in which the prowler might reveal his wickedness without disguise. Mr Pickering walked briskly along the road, then less briskly as he drew nearer the farm. An opportune belt of shrubs that ran from the gate adjoining the road to a point not far from the house gave him just the cover he needed. He slipped into this belt of shrubs and began to work his way through them.

Like generals, authors, artists, and others who, after planning broad effects, have to get down to the detail work, he found that this was where his troubles began. He had conceived the journey through the shrubbery in rather an airy mood. He thought he would just go through the shrubbery. He had not taken into account the branches, the thorns, the occasional unexpected holes, and he was both warm and dishevelled when he reached the end of it and found himself out in the open within a short distance of what he recognized as beehives. It was not for some time that he was able to give that selfless attention to exterior objects which is the prowler's chief asset. For quite a while the only thought of which he was conscious was that what he needed most was a cold drink and a cold bath. Then, with a return to clear-headedness, he realized that he was standing out in the open, visible from three sides to anyone who might be in the vicinity, and he withdrew into the shrubbery. He was not fond of the shrubbery, but it was a splendid place to withdraw into. It swallowed you up.

This was the last move of the first part of Mr Pickering's active campaign. He stayed where he was, in the middle of a bush, and waited for the enemy to do something. What he expected him to do he did not know. The subconscious thought that animated him was that on a night like this something was bound to happen sooner or later. Just such a thought on similarly stimulating nights had animated men of his acquaintance thirty years ago, men who were as elderly and stolid and unadventurous now as Mr Pickering had been then. He would have resented the suggestion profoundly, but the truth of the matter was that Dudley Pickering, after a late start, had begun to play Indians.

Nothing had happened for a long time – for such a long time that, in spite of the ferment within him, Mr Pickering almost began to believe that nothing would happen. The moon shone with unutterable calm. The crickets and the tree frogs performed their interminable duet, apparently unconscious that they were attacking it in different keys – a fact that, after a while, began to infuriate Mr Pickering. Mosquitoes added their reedy tenor to the concert. A twig on which he was standing snapped with a report like a pistol. The moon went on shining.

Away in the distance a dog began to howl. An automobile passed in the road. For a few moments Mr Pickering was able to occupy himself pleasantly with speculations as to its make; and then he became aware that something was walking down the back of his neck just beyond the point where his fingers could reach it. Discomfort enveloped Mr Pickering. At various times by day he had seen long-winged black creatures with slim waists and unpleasant faces. Could it be one of these? Or a caterpillar? Or – and the maddening thing was that he did not dare to slap at it, for who knew what desperate characters the sound might not attract?

Well, it wasn't stinging him; that was something.

A second howling dog joined the first one. A wave of sadness was apparently afflicting the canine population of the district to-night.

Mr Pickering's vitality began to ebb. He was ageing, and imagination slackened its grip. And then, just as he had begun to contemplate the possibility of abandoning the whole adventure and returning home, he was jerked back to boyhood again by the sound of voices.

He shrank farther back into the bushes. A man – The Man – was approaching, accompanied by his female associate. They passed so close to him that he could have stretched out a hand and touched them.

The female associate was speaking, and her first words set all Mr Pickering's suspicions dancing a dance of triumph. The girl gave herself away with her opening sentence.

'You can't think how nervous I was this afternoon,' he heard her say. She had a soft pleasant voice; but soft, pleasant voices may be the vehicles for conveying criminal thoughts. 'I thought every moment one of those newspaper men would look in here.'

Where was here? Ah, that outhouse! Mr Pickering had had his suspicions of that outhouse already. It was one of those structures that look at you furtively as if something were hiding in them.

'James! James! I thought I heard James in those bushes.'

The girl was looking straight at the spot occupied by Mr Pickering, and it had been the start caused by her first words and the resultant rustle of branches that had directed her attention to him. He froze. The danger passed. She went on speaking. Mr Pickering pondered on James. Who was James? Another of the gang, of course. How many of them were there?

'Once I thought it was all up. One of them was about a yard from the window, just going to look in.'

Mr Pickering thrilled. There was something hidden in the outhouse, then! Swag?

'Thank goodness, a bee stung him at the psychological moment, and – oh!'

She stopped, and The Man spoke:

'What's the matter?'

It interested Mr Pickering that The Man retained his English accent even when talking privately with his associates. For practice, no doubt.

'Come and get a banana,' said the girl. And they went off together in the direction of the house, leaving Mr Pickering bewildered. Why a banana? Was it a slang term of the underworld for a pistol? It must be that.

But he had no time for speculation. Now was his chance, the only chance he would ever get of looking into that outhouse and finding out its mysterious contents. He had seen the girl unlock the door. A few steps would take him there. All it needed was nerve. With a strong effort Mr Pickering succeeded in obtaining the nerve. He burst from his bush and trotted to the outhouse door, opened it, and looked in. And at that moment something touched his leg.

At the right time and in the right frame of mind man is capable of stoic endurances that excite wonder and admiration. Mr Pickering was no weakling. He had once upset his automobile in a ditch, and had waited for twenty minutes until help came to relieve a broken arm, and he had done it without a murmur. But on the present occasion there was a difference. His mind was not adjusted for the occurrence. There are times when it is unseasonable to touch a man on the leg. This was a moment when it was unseasonable in the case of Mr Pickering. He bounded silently into the air, his whole being rent asunder as by a cataclysm.

He had been holding his revolver in his hand as a protection against nameless terrors, and as he leaped he pulled the trigger. Then with the automatic instinct for self-preservation, he sprang back into the bushes, and began to push his way through them until he had reached a safe distance from the danger zone.

James, the cat, meanwhile, hurt at the manner in which his friendly move had been received, had taken refuge on the outhouse roof. He mewed complainingly, a puzzled note in his voice. Mr Pickering's behaviour had been one of those things that no fellow can understand. The whole thing seemed inexplicable to James.

18

LORD DAWLISH stood in the doorway of the outhouse, holding the body of Eustace gingerly by the tail. It was a solemn moment. There was no room for doubt as to the completeness of the extinction of Lady Wetherby's pet.

Dudley Pickering's bullet had done its lethal work. Eustace's adventurous career was over. He was through.

Elizabeth's mouth was trembling, and she looked very white in the moonlight. Being naturally soft-hearted, she deplored the tragedy for its own sake; and she was also, though not lacking in courage, decidedly upset by the discovery that some person unknown had been roaming her premises with a fire-arm.

'Oh, Bill!' she said. Then: 'Poor little chap!' And then: 'Who could have done it?'

Lord Dawlish did not answer. His whole mind was occupied at the moment with the contemplation of the fact that she had called him Bill. Then he realized that she had spoken three times and expected a reply.

'Who could have done it?'

Bill pondered. Never a quick thinker, the question found him unprepared.

'Some fellow, I expect,' he said at last brightly. 'Got in, don't you know, and then his pistol went off by accident.'

'But what was he doing with a pistol?'

Bill looked a little puzzled at this.

'Why, he would have a pistol, wouldn't he? I thought everybody had over here.'

Except for what he had been able to observe during the brief period of his present visit, Lord Dawlish's knowledge of the United States had been derived from the American plays which he had seen in London, and in these chappies were producing revolvers all the time. He had got the impression that a revolver was as much a part of the ordinary well-dressed man's equipment in the United States as a collar.

'I think it was a burglar,' said Elizabeth. 'There have been a lot of burglaries down here this summer.'

'Would a burglar burgle the outhouse? Rummy idea, rather, what? Not much sense in it. I think it must have been a tramp. I expect tramps are always popping about and nosing into all sorts of extraordinary places, you know.'

'He must have been standing quite close to us while we were talking,' said Elizabeth, with a shiver.

Bill looked about him. Everywhere was peace. No sinister sounds competed with the croaking of the tree frogs. No alien figures infested the landscape. The only alien figure, that of Mr Pickering, was wedged into a bush, invisible to the naked eye.

'He's gone now, at any rate,' he said. 'What are we going to do?'

Elizabeth gave another shiver as she glanced hurriedly at the deceased. After life's fitful fever Eustace slept well, but he was not looking his best.

'With – it?' she said.

'I say,' advised Bill, 'I shouldn't call him "it," don't you know. It sort of rubs it in. Why not "him"? I suppose we had better bury him. Have you a spade anywhere handy?'

'There isn't a spade on the place.'

Bill looked thoughtful.

'It takes weeks to make a hole with anything else, you know,' he said. 'When I was a kid a friend of mine bet me I wouldn't dig my way through to China with a pocket knife It was an awful frost. I tried for a couple of days, and broke the knife and didn't get anywhere near China.' He laid the remains on the grass and surveyed them meditatively. 'This is what fellows always run up against in the detective novels – What to Do With the Body. They manage the murder part of it all right, and then stub their toes on the body problem.'

'I wish you wouldn't talk as if we had done a murder.'

'I feel as if we had, don't you?'

'Exactly.'

'I read a story once where a fellow slugged somebody and melted the corpse down in a bath tub with sulphuric –'

'Stop! You're making me sick!'

'Only a suggestion, don't you know,' said Bill apologetically.

'Well, suggest something else, then.'

'How about leaving him on Lady Wetherby's doorstep? See what I mean – let them take him in with the morning milk? Or, if you would rather ring the bell and go away, and – you don't think much of it?'

'I simply haven't the nerve to do anything so risky.'

'Oh, I would do it. There would be no need for you to come.'

'I wouldn't dream of deserting you.'

'That's awfully good of you.'

'Besides, I'm not going to be left alone to-night until I can jump into my little white bed and pull the clothes over my head. I'm scared. I'm just boneless with fright. And I wouldn't go anywhere near Lady Wetherby's doorstep with it.'

'Him.'

'It's no use, I can't think of it as "him." It's no good asking me to.'

Bill frowned thoughtfully.

'I read a story once where two chappies wanted to get rid of a body. They put it inside a fellow's piano.'

'You do seem to have read the most horrible sort of books.'

'I rather like a bit of blood with my fiction,' said Bill. 'What about this piano scheme I read about?'

'People only have talking machines in these parts'

'I read a story –'

'Let's try to forget the stories you've read. Suggest something of your own.'

'Well, could we dissect the little chap?'

'Dissect him?'

'And bury him in the cellar, you know. Fellows do it to their wives.'

Elizabeth shuddered.

'Try again,' she said.

'Well, the only other thing I can think of is to take him into the woods and leave him there. It's a pity we can't let Lady Wetherby know where he is; she seems rather keen on him. But I suppose the main point is to get rid of him.'

'I know how we can do both. That's a good idea of yours about the woods. They are part of Lady Wetherby's property. I used to wander about there in the spring when the house was empty. There's a sort of shack in the middle of them. I shouldn't think anybody ever went there – it's a deserted sort of place. We could leave him there, and then – well, we might write Lady Wetherby a letter or something. We could think out that part afterward.'

'It's the best thing we've thought of. You really want to come?'

'If you attempt to leave here without me I shall scream. Let's be starting.'

Bill picked Eustace up by his convenient tail.

'I read a story once,' he said, 'where a fellow was lugging a corpse through a wood, when suddenly –'

'Stop right there,' said Elizabeth firmly.

During the conversation just recorded Dudley Pickering had been keeping a watchful eye on Bill and Elizabeth from the interior of a bush. His was not the ideal position for espionage, for he was too far off to hear what they said, and the light was too dim to enable him to see what it was that Bill was holding. It looked to Mr Pickering like a sack or bag of some sort. As time went by he became convinced that it was a sack, limp and empty at present, but destined later to receive and bulge with what he believed was technically known as the swag. When the two objects of vigilance concluded their lengthy consultation, and moved off in the direction of Lady Wetherby's woods, any doubts he may have had as to whether they were the criminals he had suspected them of being were dispersed. The whole thing worked out logically.

The Man, having spied out the land in his two visits to Lady Wetherby's house, was now about to break in. His accomplice would stand by with the sack. With a beating heart Mr Pickering gripped his revolver and moved round in the shadow of the shrubbery till he came to the gate, when he was just in time to see the guilty couple disappear into the woods. He followed them. He was glad to get on the move again. While he had been wedged into the bush, quite a lot of the bush had been wedged into him. Something sharp had pressed against the calf of his leg, and he had been pinched in a number of tender places. And he was convinced that one more of God's unpleasant creatures had got down the back of his neck.

Dudley Pickering moved through the wood as snakily as he could. Nature had shaped him more for stability than for snakiness, but he did his best. He tingled with the excitement of the chase, and endeavoured to creep through the undergrowth like one of those intelligent Indians of whom he had read so many years before in the pages of Mr Fenimore Cooper. In those days Dudley Pickering had not thought very highly of Fenimore Cooper, holding his work deficient in serious and scientific interest; but now it seemed to him that there had been something in the man after all, and he resolved to get some of his books and go over them again. He wished he had read them more carefully at the time, for they doubtless contained much information and many hints which would have come in handy just now. He seemed, for example, to recall characters in them who had the knack of going through forests without letting a single twig crack beneath their feet. Probably the author had told how this was done. In his unenlightened state it was beyond Mr Pickering. The wood seemed carpeted with twigs. Whenever he stepped he trod on one, and whenever he trod on one it cracked beneath his feet. There were moments when he felt gloomily that he might just as well be firing a machine-gun.

Bill, meanwhile, Elizabeth following close behind him, was ploughing his way onward. From time to time he would turn to administer some encouraging remark, for it had come home to him by now that encouraging remarks were what she needed very much in the present crisis of her affairs. She was showing him a new and hitherto unsuspected side of her character. The Elizabeth whom he had known – the valiant, self-reliant Elizabeth - had gone, leaving in her stead someone softer, more appealing, more approachable. It was this that was filling him with strange emotions as he led the way to their destination.

He was becoming more and more conscious of a sense of being drawn very near to Elizabeth, of a desire to soothe, comfort, and protect her. It was as if to-night he had discovered the missing key to a puzzle or the missing element in some chemical combination. Like most big men, his mind was essentially a protective mind; weakness drew out the best that was in him. And it was only to-night that Elizabeth had given any sign of having any weakness in her composition. That clear vision which had come to him on his long walk came again now, that vivid conviction that she was the only girl in the world for him.

He was debating within himself the advisability of trying to find words to express this sentiment, when Mr Pickering, the modern Chingachgook, trod on another twig in the background and Elizabeth stopped abruptly with a little cry.

'What was that?' she demanded.

Bill had heard a noise too. It was impossible to be within a dozen yards of Mr Pickering, when on the trail, and not hear a noise. The suspicion that someone was following them did not come to him, for he was a man rather of common sense than of imagination, and common sense was asking him bluntly why the deuce anybody should want to tramp after them through a wood at that time of night. He caught the note of panic in Elizabeth's voice, and was soothing her.

'It was just a branch breaking. You hear all sorts of rum noises in a wood.'

'I believe it's the man with the pistol following us!'

'Nonsense. Why should he? Silly thing to do!' He spoke almost severely.

'Look!' cried Elizabeth.

'What?'

'I saw someone dodge behind that tree.'

'You mustn't let yourself imagine things. Buck up!'

'I can't buck up. I'm scared.'

'Which tree did you think you saw someone dodge behind?'

'That big one there.'

'Well, listen: I'll go back and –'

'If you leave me for an instant I shall die in agonies.' She gulped. 'I never knew I was such a coward before I'm just a worm.'

'Nonsense. This sort of thing might frighten anyone. I read a story once –'

'Don't!'

Bill found that his heart had suddenly begun to beat with unaccustomed rapidity. The desire to soothe, comfort, and protect Elizabeth became the immediate ambition of his life. It was very dark where they stood. The moonlight, which fell in little patches round them, did not penetrate the thicket which they had entered. He could hardly see her. He was merely aware of her as a presence. An excellent idea occurred to him.

'Hold my hand,' he said.

It was what he would have said to a frightened child, and there was much of the frightened child about Elizabeth then. The Eustace mystery had given her a shock which subsequent events had done nothing to dispel, and she had lost that jauntiness and self-confidence which was her natural armour against the more ordinary happenings of life.

Something small and soft slid gratefully into his palm, and there was silence for a space. Bill said nothing. Elizabeth said nothing. And Mr Pickering had stopped treading on twigs. The faintest of night breezes ruffled the tree-tops above them. The moonbeams filtered through the branches. He held her hand tightly.

'Better?'

'Much.'

The breeze died away. Not a leaf stirred. The wood was very still. Somewhere on a bough a bird moved drowsily 'All right?'

'Yes.'

And then something happened – something shattering, disintegrating. It was only a pheasant, but it sounded like the end of the world. It rose at their feet with a rattle that filled the universe, and for a moment all was black confusion. And when that moment had passed it became apparent to Bill that his arm was round Elizabeth, that she was sobbing helplessly, and that he was kissing her. Somebody was talking very rapidly in a low voice.

He found that it was himself.

'Elizabeth!'

There was something wonderful about the name, a sort of music. This was odd, because the name, as a name, was far from being a favourite of his. Until that moment childish associations had prejudiced him against it. It had been inextricably involved in his mind with an atmosphere of stuffy schoolrooms and general misery, for it had been his misfortune that his budding mind was constitutionally incapable of remembering who had been Queen of England at the time of the Spanish Armada – a fact that had caused a good deal of friction with a rather sharp-tempered governess. But now it seemed the only possible name for a girl to have, the only label that could even remotely suggest those feminine charms which he found in this girl beside him. There was poetry in every syllable of it. It was like one of those deep chords which fill the hearer with vague yearnings for strange and beautiful things. He asked for nothing better than to stand here repeating it.

'Elizabeth!'

'Bill, dear!'

That sounded good too. There was music in 'Bill' when properly spoken. The reason why all the other Bills in the world had got the impression that it was a prosaic sort of name was that there was only one girl in existence capable of speaking it properly, and she was not for them.

'Bill, are you really fond of me?'

'Fond of you!'

She gave a sigh. 'You're so splendid!'

Bill was staggered. These were strange words. He had never thought much of himself. He had always looked on himself as rather a chump – well-meaning, perhaps, but an awful ass. It seemed incredible that any one – and Elizabeth of all people – could look on him as splendid.

And yet the very fact that she had said it gave it a plausible sort of sound. It shook his convictions. Splendid! Was he? By Jove, perhaps he was, what? Rum idea, but it grew on a chap. Filled with a novel feeling of exaltation, he kissed Elizabeth eleven times in rapid succession.

He felt devilish fit. He would have liked to run a mile or two and jump a few gates. He wished five or six starving beggars would come along; it would be pleasant to give the poor blighters money. It was too much to expect at that time of night, of course, but it would be rather jolly if Jess Willard would roll up and try to pick a quarrel. He would show him something. He felt grand and strong and full of beans. What a ripping thing life was when you came to think of it.

'This,' he said, 'is perfectly extraordinary!' And time stood still.

A sense of something incongruous jarred upon Bill. Something seemed to be interfering with the supreme romance of that golden moment. It baffled him at first. Then he realized that he was still holding Eustace by the tail.

Dudley Pickering had watched these proceedings – as well as the fact that it was extremely dark and that he was endeavouring to hide a portly form behind a slender bush would permit him – with a sense of bewilderment. A comic artist drawing Mr Pickering at that moment would no doubt have placed above his head one of those large marks of interrogation which lend vigour and snap to modern comic art. Certainly such a mark of interrogation would have summed up his feelings exactly. Of what was taking place he had not the remotest notion. All he knew was that for some inexplicable reason his quarry had come to a halt and seemed to have settled down for an indefinite stay. Voices came to him in an indistinguishable murmur, intensely irritating to a conscientious tracker. One of Fenimore Cooper's Indians – notably Chingachgook, if, which seemed incredible, that was really the man's name – would have crept up without a sound and heard what was being said and got in on the ground floor of whatever plot was being hatched. But experience had taught Mr Pickering that, superior as he was to Chingachgook and his friends in many ways, as a creeper he was not in their class. He weighed thirty or forty pounds more than a first-class creeper should. Besides, creeping is like golf. You can't take it up in the middle forties and expect to compete with those who have been at it from infancy.

He had resigned himself to an all-night vigil behind the bush, when to his great delight he perceived that things had begun to move again. There was a rustling of feet in the undergrowth, and he could just see two indistinct forms making their way among the bushes. He came out of his hiding place and followed stealthily, or as stealthily as the fact that he had not even taken a correspondence course in creeping allowed. And profiting by earlier mistakes, he did succeed in making far less noise than before. In place of his former somewhat elephantine method of progression he adopted a species of shuffle which had excellent results, for it enabled him to brush twigs away instead of stepping flatfootedly on them. The new method was slow, but it had no other disadvantages.

Because it was slow, Mr Pickering was obliged to follow his prey almost entirely by ear. It was easy at first, for they seemed to be hurrying on regardless of noise. Then unexpectedly the sounds of their passage ceased.

He halted. In his boyish way the first thing he thought was that it was an ambush. He had a vision of that large man suspecting his presence and lying in wait for him with a revolver. This was not a comforting thought. Of course, if a man is going to fire a revolver at you it makes little difference whether he is a giant or a pygmy, but Mr Pickering was in no frame of mind for nice reasoning. It was the thought of Bill's physique which kept him standing there irresolute.

What would Chingachgook – assuming, for purposes of argument, that any sane godfather could really have given a helpless child a name like that – have done? He would, Mr Pickering considered, after giving the matter his earnest attention, have made a *détour* and outflanked the enemy. An excellent solution of the difficulty. Mr Pickering turned to the left and began to advance circuitously, with the result that, before he knew what he was doing, he came out into a clearing and understood the meaning of the sudden silence which had perplexed him. Footsteps made no sound on this mossy turf.

He knew where he was now; the clearing was familiar. This was where Lord Wetherby's shack-studio stood; and there it was, right in front of him, black and clear in the moonlight. And the two dark figures were going into it.

Mr Pickering retreated into the shelter of the bushes and mused upon this thing. It seemed to him that for centuries he had been doing nothing but retreat into bushes for this purpose. His perplexity had returned. He could imagine no reason why burglars should want to visit Lord Wetherby's studio. He had taken it for granted, when he had tracked them to the clearing, that they were on their way to the house, which was quite close to the shack, separated from it only by a thin belt of trees and a lawn.

They had certainly gone in. He had seen them with his own eyes – first the man, then very close behind him, apparently holding to his coat, the girl. But why?

Creep up and watch them? Would Chingachgook have taken a risk like that? Hardly, unless insured with some good company. Then what? He was still undecided when he perceived the objects of his attention emerging. He backed a little farther into the bushes.

They stood for an instant, listening apparently. The man no longer carried the sack. They exchanged a few inaudible words. Then they crossed the clearing and entered the wood a few yards to his right. He could hear the crackling of their footsteps diminishing in the direction of the road.

A devouring curiosity seized upon Mr Pickering. He wanted, more than he had wanted almost anything before in his life, to find out what the dickens they had been up to in there. He listened. The footsteps were no longer audible. He ran across the clearing and into the shack. It was then that he discovered that he had no matches.

This needless infliction, coming upon him at the crisis of an adventurous night, infuriated Mr Pickering. He swore softly. He groped round the walls for an electric-light switch, but the shack had no electric-light switch. When there was need to illuminate it an oil lamp performed the duty This occurred to Mr Pickering after he had been round the place three times, and he ceased to grope for a switch and began to seek for a match-box. He was still seeking it when he was frozen in his tracks by the sound of footsteps, muffled but by their nearness audible, just outside the door. He pulled out his pistol, which he had replaced in his pocket, backed against the wall, and stood there prepared to sell his life dearly.

The door opened.

One reads of desperate experiences ageing people in a single night. His present predicament aged Mr Pickering in a single minute. In the brief interval of time between the opening of the door and the moment when a voice outside began to speak he became a full thirty years older. His boyish ardour slipped from him, and he was once more the Dudley Pickering whom the world knew, the staid and respectable middle-aged man of affairs, who would have given a million dollars not to have got himself mixed up in this deplorable business.

And then the voice spoke.

'I'll light the lamp,' it said; and with an overpowering feeling of relief Mr Pickering recognized it as Lord Wetherby's. A moment later the temperamental peer's dapper figure became visible in silhouette against a background of pale light.

'Ah-hum!' said Mr Pickering.

The effect on Lord Wetherby was remarkable. To hear some one clear his throat at the back of a dark room, where there should rightfully be no throat to be cleared, would cause even your man of stolid habit a passing thrill. The thing got right in among Lord Wetherby's highly sensitive ganglions like an earthquake. He uttered a strangled cry, then dashed out and slammed the door behind him.

'There's someone in there!'

Lady Wetherby's tranquil voice made itself heard.

'Nonsense; who could be in there?'

'I heard him, I tell you. He growled at me!'

It seemed to Mr Pickering that the time had come to relieve the mental distress which he was causing his host. He raised his voice.

'It's all right!' he called.

'There!' said Lord Wetherby.

'Who's that?' asked Lady Wetherby, through the door.

'It's all right. It's me – Pickering.'

The door was opened a few inches by a cautious hand.

'Is that you, Pickering?'

'Yes. It's all right.'

'Don't keep saying it's all right,' said Lord Wetherby,

irritably. 'It isn't all right. What do you mean by hiding in the dark and popping out and barking at a man? You made me bite my tongue. I've never had such a shock in my life.'

Mr Pickering left his lair and came out into the open. Lord Wetherby was looking aggrieved, Lady Wetherby peacefully inquisitive. For the first time Mr Pickering discovered that Claire was present. She was standing behind Lady Wetherby with a floating white something over her head, looking very beautiful.

'For the love of Mike!' said Lady Wetherby.

Mr Pickering became aware that he was still holding the revolver.

'Oh, ah!' he said, and pocketed the weapon.

'Barking at people!' muttered Lord Wetherby in a querulous undertone.

'What on earth are you doing, Dudley?' said Claire.

There was a note in her voice which both puzzled and pained Mr Pickering, a note that seemed to suggest that she found herself in imperfect sympathy with him. Her expression deepened the suggestion. It was a cold expression, unfriendly, as if it was not so keen a pleasure to Claire to look at him as it should be for a girl to look at the man whom she is engaged to marry. He had noticed the same note in her voice and the same hostile look in her eye earlier in the evening. He had found her alone, reading a letter which, as the stamp on the envelope showed, had come from England. She had seemed so upset that he had asked her if it contained bad news, and she had replied in the negative with so much irritation that he had desisted from inquiries. But his own idea was that she had had bad news from home. Mr Pickering still clung to his early impression that her little brother Percy was consumptive, and he thought the child must have taken a turn for the worse. It was odd that she should have looked and spoken like that then, and it was odd that she should look and speak like that now. He had been vaguely disturbed then and he was vaguely disturbed now. He had the feeling that all was not well.

'Yes,' said Lady Wetherby. 'What on earth are you doing, Dudley?'

'Popping out!' grumbled Lord Wetherby.

'We came here to see Algie's picture, which has got something wrong with its eyes apparently, and we find you hiding in the dark with a gun. What's the idea?'

'It's a long story,' said Mr Pickering.

'We have the night before us,' said Lady Wetherby. 'You remember The Man – the fellow I found looking in at the window, The Man who said he knew Claire?'

'You've got that man on the brain, Dudley. What's he been doing to you now?'

'I tracked him here.'

'Tracked him? Where from?'

'From that bee-farm place where he's living. He and that girl you spoke of went into these woods. I thought they were making for the house, but they went into the shack.'

'What did they do then?' asked Lady Wetherby

'They came out again.'

'Why?'

'That's what I was trying to find out.'

Lord Wetherby uttered an exclamation.

'By Jove!' There was apprehension in his voice, but mingled with it a certain pleased surprise. 'Perhaps they were after my picture. I'll light the lamp. Good Lord, picture thieves – Romneys – missing Gainsboroughs –' His voice trailed off as he found the lamp and lit it. Relief and disappointment were nicely blended in his next words: 'No, it's still there.'

The soft light of the lamp filled the studio.

'Well, that's a comfort,' said Lady Wetherby, sauntering in. 'We couldn't afford to lose – Oh!'

Lord Wetherby spun round as her scream burst upon his already tortured nerve centres. Lady Wetherby was kneeling on the floor. Claire hurried in.

'What is it, Polly?'

Lady Wetherby rose to her feet, and pointed. Her face had lost its look of patient amusement. It was hard and set. She eyed Mr Pickering in a menacing way.

'Look!'

Claire followed her finger.

'Good gracious! It's Eustace!'

'Shot!'

She was looking intently at Mr Pickering. 'Well, Dudley,' she said, coldly, 'what about it?'

Mr Pickering found that they were all looking at him – Lady Wetherby with glittering eyes, Claire with cool scorn, Lord Wetherby with a horror which he seemed to have achieved with something of an effort.

'Well!' said Claire.

'What about it, Dudley?' said Lady Wetherby.

'I must say, Pickering,' said Lord Wetherby, 'much as I disliked the animal, it's a bit thick!'

Mr Pickering recoiled from their accusing gaze.

'Good heavens! Do you think I did it?'

In the midst of his anguish there flashed across his mind the recollection of having seen just this sort of situation in a moving picture, and of having thought it far-fetched.

Lady Wetherby's good-tempered mouth, far from good-tempered now, curled in a devastating sneer. She was looking at him as Claire, in the old days when they had toured England together in road companies, had sometimes seen her look at recalcitrant landladies. The landladies, without exception, had wilted beneath that gaze, and Mr Pickering wilted now.

'But – but – but –' was all he could contrive to say.

'Why should we think you did it?' said Lady Wetherby, bitterly. 'You had a grudge against the poor brute for biting you. We find you hiding here with a pistol and a story about burglars which an infant couldn't swallow. I suppose you thought that, if you planted the poor creature's body here, it would be up to Algie to get rid of it, and that if he were found with it I should think that it was he who had killed the animal.'

The look of horror which Lord Wetherby had managed to assume became genuine at these words. The gratitude which he had been feeling towards Mr Pickering for having removed one of the chief trials of his existence vanished.

'Great Scot!' he cried. 'So that was the game, was it?'

Mr Pickering struggled for speech. This was a nightmare.

'But I didn't! I didn't! I didn't! I tell you I hadn't the remotest notion the creature was there.'

'Oh, come, Pickering!' said Lord Wetherby. 'Come, come, come!'

Mr Pickering found that his accusers were ebbing away. Lady Wetherby had gone. Claire had gone. Only Lord Wetherby remained, looking at him like a pained groom. He dashed from the place and followed his hostess, speaking incoherently of burglars, outhouses, and misunderstandings. He even mentioned Chingachgook. But Lady Wetherby would not listen. Nobody would listen.

He found Lord Wetherby at his side, evidently prepared to go deeper into the subject. Lord Wetherby was looking now like a groom whose favourite horse has kicked him in the stomach.

'Wouldn't have thought it of you, Pickering,' said Lord Wetherby. Mr Pickering found no words. 'Wouldn't, honestly. Low trick!'

'But I tell you –'

'Devilish low trick!' repeated Lord Wetherby, with a shake of the head. 'Laws of hospitality – eaten our bread and salt, what! – all that sort of thing – kill valuable monkey – not done, you know – low, very low!'

And he followed his wife, now in full retreat, with scorn and repulsion written in her very walk.

'Mr Pickering!'

It was Claire. She stood there, holding something towards him, something that glittered in the moonlight. Her voice was hard, and the expression on her face suggested that in her estimation he was a particularly low-grade worm, one of the submerged tenth of the worm world.

'Eh?' said Mr Pickering, dazedly.

He looked at what she had in her hand, but it conveyed nothing to his overwrought mind.

'Take it!'

'Eh?'

Claire stamped.

'Very well,' she said.

She flung something on the ground before him — a small, sparkling object. Then she swept away, his eyes following her, and was lost in the darkness of the trees. Mechanically Mr Pickering stooped to pick up what she had let fall He recognized it now. It was her engagement ring.

19

BILL leaned his back against the gate that separated the grounds of the bee-farm from the high road and mused pleasantly. He was alone. Elizabeth was walking up the drive on her way to the house to tell the news to Nutty. James, the cat, who had come down from the roof of the outhouse, was sharpening his claws on a neighbouring tree. After the whirl of excitement that had been his portion for the past few hours, the peace of it all appealed strongly to Bill. It suited the mood of quiet happiness which was upon him.

Quietly happy, that was how he felt now that it was all over. The white heat of emotion had subsided to a gentle glow of contentment conducive to thought. He thought tenderly of Elizabeth. She had turned to wave her hand before going into the house, and he was still smiling fatuously. Wonderful girl! Lucky chap he was! Rum, the way they had come together! Talk about Fate, what?

He stooped to tickle James, who had finished stropping his claws and was now enjoying a friction massage against his leg, and began to brood on the inscrutable way of Fate.

Rum thing, Fate! Most extraordinary!

Suppose he had never gone down to Marvis Bay that time. He had wavered between half a dozen places; it was pure chance that he had chosen Marvis Bay. If he hadn't he would never have met old Nutcombe. Probably old Nutcombe had wavered between half a dozen places too. If they hadn't both happened to choose Marvis Bay they would never have met. And if they hadn't been the only visitors there they might never have got to know each other. And if old Nutcombe hadn't happened to slice his approach shots he would never have put him under an obligation. Queer old buster, old Nutcombe, leaving a fellow he hardly knew from Adam a cool million quid just because he cured him of slicing.

It was at this point in his meditations that it suddenly occurred to Bill that he had not yet given a thought to what was immeasurably the most important of any of the things that ought to be occupying his mind just now. What was he to do about this Lord Dawlish business?

Life at Brookport had so accustomed him to being plain Bill Chalmers that it had absolutely slipped his mind that he was really Lord Dawlish, the one man in the world whom Elizabeth looked on as an enemy. What on earth was he to do about that? Tell her? But if he told her, wouldn't she chuck him on the spot?

This was awful. The dreamy sense of well-being left him. He straightened himself to face this problem, ignoring the hint of James, who was weaving circles about his legs expectant of more tickling. A man cannot spend his time tickling cats when he has to concentrate on a dilemma of this kind.

Suppose he didn't tell her? How would that work out? Was a marriage legal if the cove who was being married went through it under a false name? He seemed to remember seeing a melodrama in his boyhood the plot of which turned on that very point. Yes, it began to come back to him. An unpleasant bargee with a black moustache had said, 'This woman is not your wife!' and caused the dickens of a lot of unpleasantness; but there in its usual slipshod way memory failed. Had subsequent events proved the bargee right or wrong? It was a question for a lawyer to decide. Jerry Nichols would know. Well, there was plenty of time, thank goodness, to send Jerry Nichols a cable, asking for his professional opinion, and to get the straight tip long before the wedding day arrived.

Laying this part of it aside for the moment, and assuming that the thing could be worked, what about the money? Like a chump, he had told Elizabeth on the first day of his visit that he hadn't any money except what he made out of his job as secretary of the club. He couldn't suddenly spring five million dollars on her and pretend that he had forgotten all about it till then.

Of course, he could invent an imaginary uncle or something, and massacre him during the honeymoon. Something in that. He pictured the thing in his mind. Breakfast: Elizabeth doling out the scrambled eggs. 'What's the matter, Bill? Why did you exclaim like that? Is there some bad news in the letter you are reading?' 'Oh, it's nothing – only my Uncle John's died and left me five million dollars.'

The scene worked out so well that his mind became a little above itself. It suggested developments of serpentine craftiness. Why not get Jerry Nichols to write him a letter about his Uncle John and the five millions? Jerry liked doing that sort of thing. He would do it like a shot, and chuck in a lot of legal words to make it sound right. It began to be clear to Bill that any move he took – except full confession, at which he jibbed – was going to involve Jerry Nichols as an ally; and this discovery had a soothing effect on him. It made him feel that the responsibility had been shifted. He couldn't do anything till he had consulted Jerry, so there was no use in worrying. And, being one of those rare persons who can cease worrying instantly when they have convinced themselves that it is useless, he dismissed the entire problem from his mind and returned to the more congenial occupation of thinking of Elizabeth.

It was a peculiar feature of his position that he found himself unable to think of Elizabeth without thinking of Claire. He tried to, but failed. Every virtue in Elizabeth seemed to call up the recollection of a corresponding defect in Claire It became almost mathematical. Elizabeth was so straight on the level they called it over here. Claire was a corkscrew among women. Elizabeth was sunny and cheerful. Querulousness was Claire's besetting sin. Elizabeth was such a pal. Claire had never been that. The effect that Claire had always had on him was to deepen the conviction, which never really left him, that he was a bit of an ass. Elizabeth, on the other hand, bucked him up and made him feel as if he really amounted to something.

How different they were! Their very voices – Elizabeth had a sort of quiet, soothing, pleasant voice, the kind of voice that somehow suggested that she thought a lot of a chap without her having to say it in so many words. Whereas Claire's voice – he had noticed it right from the beginning – Claire's voice –

While he was trying to make clear to himself just what it was about Claire's voice that he had not liked he was granted the opportunity of analysing by means of direct observation its failure to meet his vocal ideals, for at this moment it spoke behind him.

'Bill!'

She was standing in the road, her head still covered with that white, filmy something which had commended itself to Mr Pickering's eyes. She was looking at him in a way that seemed somehow to strike a note of appeal. She conveyed an atmosphere of softness and repentance, a general suggestion of prodigal daughters revisiting old homesteads.

'We seem always to be meeting at gates, don't we?' she said, with a faint smile.

It was a deprecating smile, wistful.

'Bill!' she said again, and stopped. She laid her left hand lightly on the gate. Bill had a sort of impression that there was some meaning behind this action; that, if he were less of a chump than Nature had made him, he would at this point receive some sort of a revelation. But, being as Nature had made him, he did not get it.

He was one of those men to whom a girl's left hand is simply a girl's left hand, irrespective of whether it wears rings on its third finger or not.

This having become evident to Claire after a moment of silence, she withdrew her hand in rather a disappointed way and prepared to attack the situation from another angle.

'Bill, I've come to say something to you.'

Bill was looking at her curiously. He could not have believed that, even after what had happened, he could face her with such complete detachment; that she could so extraordinarily not matter. He felt no resentment toward her. It was simply that she had gone out of his life.

'Bill, I've been a fool.'

He made no reply to this for he could think of no reply that was sufficiently polite. 'Yes?' sounded as if he meant to say that that was just what he had expected. 'Really?' had a sarcastic ring. He fell back on facial expression, to imply that he was interested and that she might tell all.

Claire looked away down the road and began to speak in a low, quick voice:

'I've been a fool all along. I lost you through being a fool. When I saw you dancing with that girl in the restaurant I didn't stop to think. I was angry. I was jealous. I ought to have trusted you, but – Oh, well, I was a fool.'

'My dear girl, you had a perfect right –'

'I hadn't. I was an idiot. Bill, I've come to ask you if you can't forgive me.'

'I wish you wouldn't talk like that – there's nothing to forgive.'

The look which Claire gave him in answer to this was meek and affectionate, but inwardly she was wishing that she could bang his head against the gate. His slowness was maddening. Long before this he should have leaped into the road in order to fold her in his arms. Her voice shook with the effort she had to make to keep it from sharpness.

'I mean, is it too late? I mean, can you really forgive me? Oh, Bill' – she stopped herself by the fraction of a second from adding 'you idiot' – 'can't we be the same again to each other? Can't we – pretend all this has never happened?'

Exasperating as Bill's wooden failure to play the scene in the spirit in which her imagination had conceived it was to Claire, several excuses may be offered for him: He had opened the evening with a shattering blow at his faith in woman. He had walked twenty miles at a rapid pace. He had heard shots and found a corpse, and carried the latter by the tail across country. Finally, he had had the stunning shock of discovering that Elizabeth Boyd loved him. He was not himself. He found a difficulty in concentrating. With the result that, in answer to this appeal from a beautiful girl whom he had once imagined that he loved, all he could find to say was: 'How do you mean?'

Claire, never an adept at patience, just succeeded in swallowing the remark that sprang into her mind. It was incredible to her that a man could exist who had so little intuition. She had not anticipated the necessity of being compelled to put the substance of her meaning in so many blunt words, but it seemed that only so could she make him understand.

'I mean, can't we be engaged again, Bill?'

Bill's overtaxed brain turned one convulsive hand-spring, and came to rest with a sense of having dislocated itself. This was too much. This was not right. No fellow at the end of a hard evening ought to have to grapple with this sort of thing. What on earth did she mean, springing questions like that on him? How could they be engaged? She was going to marry someone else, and so was he. Something of these thoughts he managed to put into words:

'But you're engaged to –'

'I've broken my engagement with Mr Pickering.'

'Great Scot! When?'

'To-night. I found out his true character. He is cruel and treacherous. Something happened – it may sound nothing to you, but it gave me an insight into what he really was. Polly Wetherby had a little monkey, and just because it bit Mr Pickering he shot it.'

'Pickering!'

'Yes. He wasn't the sort of man I should have expected to do a mean, cruel thing like that. It sickened me. I gave him back his ring then and there. Oh, what a relief it was! What a fool I was ever to have got engaged to such a man.'

Bill was puzzled. He was one of those simple men who take their fellows on trust, but who, if once that trust is shattered, can never recover it. Like most simple men, he was tenacious of ideas when he got them, and the belief that Claire was playing fast and loose was not lightly to be removed from his mind. He had found her out during his self-communion that night, and he could never believe her again. He had the feeling that there was something behind what she was saying. He could not put his finger on the clue, but that there was a clue he was certain.

'I only got engaged to him out of pique. I was angry with you, and – Well, that's how it happened.'

Still Bill could not believe. It was plausible. It sounded true. And yet some instinct told him that it was not true. And while he waited, perplexed, Claire made a false step.

The thing had been so close to the top of her mind ever since she had come to the knowledge of it that it had been hard for her to keep it down. Now she could keep it down no longer.

'How wonderful about old Mr Nutcombe, Bill!' she said.

A vast relief rolled over Bill. Despite his instinct, he had been wavering. But now he understood. He had found the clue.

'You got my letter, then?'

'Yes; it was forwarded on from the theatre. I got it to-night.'

Too late she realized what she had said and the construction that an intelligent man would put on it. Then she reflected that Bill was not an intelligent man. She shot a swift glance at him. To all appearances he had suspected nothing.

'It went all over the place,' she hurried on. 'The people at the Portsmouth theatre sent it to the London office, who sent it home, and mother mailed it on to me.'

'I see.'

There was a silence. Claire drew a step nearer.

'Bill!' she said softly.

Bill shut his eyes. The moment had come which he had dreaded. Not even the thought that she was crooked, that she had been playing with him, could make it any better. She was a woman and he was a man. That was all that mattered, and nothing could alter it.

'I'm sorry,' he said. 'It's impossible.'

Claire stared at him in amazement. She had not been prepared for this. He met her eyes, but every nerve in his body was protesting.

'Bill!'

'I'm sorry.'

'But, Bill!'

He set his teeth. It was just as bad as he had thought it would be.

'But, Bill, I've explained. I've told you how –'

'I know.'

Claire's eyes opened wide.

'I thought you loved me.' She came closer. She pulled at his sleeve. Her voice took on a note of soft raillery. 'Don't be absurd, Bill! You mustn't behave like a sulky schoolboy. It isn't like you, this. You surely don't want me to humble myself more than I have done.' She gave a little laugh. 'Why, Bill, I'm proposing to you! I know I've treated you badly, but I've explained why. You must be just enough to see that it wasn't altogether my fault. I'm only human. And if I made a mistake I've done all I can do to undo it. I –'

'Claire, listen: I'm engaged!'

She fell back. For the first time the sense of defeat came to her. She had anticipated many things. She had looked for difficulties. But she had not expected this. A feeling of cold fury surged over her at the way fate had tricked her. She had gambled recklessly on her power of fascination, and she had lost.

Mr Pickering, at that moment brooding in solitude in the smoking-room of Lady Wetherby's house, would have been relieved could he have known how wistfully she was thinking of him.

'You're engaged?'

'Yes.'

'Well!' She forced another laugh. 'How very – rapid of you! To whom?'

'To Elizabeth Boyd.'

'I'm afraid I'm very ignorant, but who is Elizabeth Boyd? The ornate lady you were dancing with at the restaurant?'

'No!'

'Who then?'

'She is old Ira Nutcombe's niece. The money ought to have been left to her. That was why I came over to America, to see if I could do anything for her.'

'And you're going to marry her? How very romantic – and convenient! What an excellent arrangement for her. Which of you suggested it?'

Bill drew in a deep breath. All this was, he supposed, unavoidable, but it was not pleasant.

Claire suddenly abandoned her pose of cool amusement. The fire behind it blazed through.

'You fool!' she cried passionately. 'Are you blind? Can't you see that this girl is simply after your money? A child could see it.'

Bill looked at her steadily.

'You're quite wrong. She doesn't know who I am.'

'Doesn't know who you are? What do you mean? She must know by this time that her uncle left his money to you.'

'But she doesn't know that I am Lord Dawlish. I came to America under another name. She knows me as Chalmers.'

Claire was silent for a moment.

'How did you get to know her?' she asked, more quietly.

'I met her brother by chance in New York.'

'By chance!'

'Quite by chance. A man I knew in England lent me his rooms in New York. He happened to be a friend of Boyd's. Boyd came to call on him one night, and found me.'

'Odd! Had your mutual friend been away from New York long?'

'Some months.'

'And in all that time Mr Boyd had not discovered that he had left. They must have been great friends! What happened then?'

'Boyd invited me down here.'

'Down here?'

'They live in this house.'

'Is Miss Boyd the girl who keeps the bee-farm?'

'She is.'

Claire's eyes suddenly lit up. She began to speak in a louder voice:

'Bill, you're an infant, a perfect infant! Of course, she's after your money. Do you really imagine for one instant that this Elizabeth Boyd of yours and her brother don't know as well as I do that you are really Lord Dawlish? I always thought you

157

had a trustful nature! You tell me the brother met you by chance. Chance! And invited you down here. I bet he did! He knew his business! And now you're going to marry the girl so that they will get the money after all! Splendid! Oh, Bill, you're a wonderful, wonderful creature! Your innocence is touching.'

She swung round.

'Good night,' she called over her shoulder.

He could hear her laughing as she went down the road.

20

In the smoking-room of Lady Wetherby's house, chewing the dead stump of a once imposing cigar, Dudley Pickering sat alone with his thoughts. He had been alone for half an hour now. Once Lord Wetherby had looked in, to withdraw at once coldly, with the expression of a groom who has found loathsome things in the harness-room. Roscoe Sherriff, good, easy man, who could never dislike people, no matter what they had done, had come for a while to bear him company; but Mr Pickering's society was not for the time being entertaining. He had answered with grunts the Press-agent's kindly attempts at conversation, and the latter had withdrawn to seek a more congenial audience. And now Mr Pickering was alone, talking things over with his subconscious self.

A man's subconscious self is not the ideal companion. It lurks for the greater part of his life in some dark den of its own, hidden away, and emerges only to taunt and deride and increase the misery of a miserable hour. Mr Pickering's rare interviews with his subconscious self had happened until now almost entirely in the small hours of the night, when it had popped out to remind him, as he lay sleepless, that all flesh was grass and that he was not getting any younger. To-night, such had been the shock of the evening's events, it came to him at a time which was usually his happiest – the time that lay between dinner and bed. Mr Pickering at that point of the day was generally feeling his best. But to-night was different from the other nights of his life.

One may picture Subconscious Self as a withered, cynical, malicious person standing before Mr Pickering and regarding him with an evil smile. There has been a pause, and now Subconscious Self speaks again:

'You will have to leave to-morrow. Couldn't possibly stop on after what's happened. Now you see what comes of behaving like a boy.'

Mr Pickering writhed.

'Made a pretty considerable fool of yourself, didn't you, with your revolvers and your hidings and your trailings? Too old for that sort of thing, you know. You're getting on. Probably have a touch of lumbago to-morrow. You must remember you aren't a youngster. Got to take care of yourself. Next time you feel an impulse to hide in shrubberies and take moonlight walks through damp woods, perhaps you will listen to me.'

Mr Pickering relit the stump of his cigar defiantly and smoked in long gulps for a while. He was trying to persuade himself that all this was untrue, but it was not easy. The cigar became uncomfortably hot, and he threw it away. He fumbled in his waistcoat pocket and produced a diamond ring, at which he looked pensively.

'A pretty thing, is it not?' said Subconscious Self

Mr Pickering sighed. That moment when Claire had thrown the ring at his feet and swept out of his life like an offended queen had been the culminating blow of a night of blows, the knock-out following on a series of minor punches. Subconscious Self seized the opportunity to become offensive again.

'You've lost her, all through your own silly fault,' it said. 'How on earth you can have been such a perfect fool beats me. Running round with a gun like a boy of fourteen! Well, it's done now and it can't be mended. Countermand the order for cake, send a wire putting off the wedding, dismiss the bridesmaids, tell the organist he can stop practising "The Voice that Breathed O'er Eden" – no wedding-bells for you! For Dudley Damfool Pickering, Esquire, the lonely hearth for evermore! Little feet pattering about the house? Not on your life! Childish voices sticking up the old man for half a dollar to buy candy? No, sir! Not for D. Bonehead Pickering, the amateur trailing arbutus!'

Subconscious Self may have had an undesirable way of expressing itself, but there was no denying the truth of what it said. Its words carried conviction. Mr Pickering replaced the ring in his pocket, and, burying his head in his hands, groaned in bitterness of spirit.

He had lost her. He must face the fact. She had thrown him over. Never now would she sit at his table, the brightest jewel of Detroit's glittering social life. She would have made a stir in Detroit. Now that city would never know her Not that he was worrying much about Detroit. He was worrying about himself. How could he ever live without her?

This mood of black depression endured for a while, and then Mr Pickering suddenly became aware that Subconscious Self was sneering at him. 'You're a wonder!' said Subconscious Self.

'What do you mean?'

'Why, trying to make yourself think that at the bottom of your heart you aren't tickled to death that this has happened. You know perfectly well that you're tremendously relieved that you haven't got to marry the girl after all. You can fool everybody else, but you can't fool me. You're delighted, man, delighted!'

The mere suggestion revolted Mr Pickering. He was on the point of indignant denial, when quite abruptly there came home to him the suspicion that the statement was not so preposterous after all. It seemed incredible and indecent that such a thing should be, but he could not deny, now that it was put to him point-blank in this way, that a certain sense of relief was beginning to mingle itself with his gloom. It was shocking to realize, but – yes, he actually was feeling as if he had escaped from something which he had dreaded. Half an hour ago there had been no suspicion of such an emotion among the many which had occupied his attention, but now he perceived it clearly. Half an hour ago he had felt like Lucifer hurled from heaven. Now, though how that train of thought had started he could not have said, he was distinctly conscious of the silver lining. Subconscious Self began to drive the thing home.

'Be honest with yourself,' it said. 'You aren't often. No man is. Look at the matter absolutely fairly. You know perfectly well that the mere idea of marriage has always scared you. You hate making yourself conspicuous in public. Think what it would be like, standing up there in front of all the world and getting married. And then – afterwards! Why on earth do you think that you would have been happy with this girl? What do you know about her except that she is a beauty? I grant you she's that, but are you aware of the infinitesimal part looks play in married life? My dear chap, better is it for a man that he marry a sympathetic gargoyle than a Venus with a streak of hardness in her. You know – and you would admit it if you were honest with yourself – that this girl is hard. She's got a chilled-steel soul.

'If you wanted to marry some one – and there's no earthly reason why you should, for your life's perfectly full and happy with your work – this is the last girl you ought to marry. You're a middle-aged man. You're set. You like life to jog along at a peaceful walk. This girl wants it to be a fox-trot. You've got habits which you have had for a dozen years. I ask you, is she the sort of girl to be content to be a stepmother to a middle-aged man's habits? Of course, if you were really in love with her, if she were your mate, and all that sort of thing, you would take a pleasure in making yourself over to suit her requirements. But you aren't in love with her. You are simply caught by her looks. I tell you, you ought to look on that moment when she gave you back your ring as the luckiest moment of your life. You ought to make a sort of anniversary of it. You ought to endow a hospital or something out of pure gratitude. I don't know how long you're going to live – if you act like a grown-up man instead of a boy and keep out of woods and shrubberies at night you may live for ever – but you will never have a greater bit of luck than the one that happened to you to-night.'

Mr Pickering was convinced. His spirits soared. Marriage! What was marriage? Slavery, not to be endured by your man of spirit. Look at all the unhappy marriages you saw everywhere.

Besides, you had only to recall some of the novels and plays of recent years to get the right angle on marriage. According to the novelists and playwrights, shrewd fellows who knew what was what, if you talked to your wife about your business she said you had no soul; if you didn't, she said you didn't think enough of her to let her share your life. If you gave her expensive presents and an unlimited credit account, she complained that you looked on her as a mere doll; and if you didn't, she called you a screw. That was marriage. If it didn't get you with the left jab, it landed on you with the right upper-cut. None of that sort of thing for Dudley Pickering.

'You're absolutely right,' he said, enthusiastically. 'Funny I never looked at it that way before.'

Somebody was turning the door-handle. He hoped it was Roscoe Sherriff. He had been rather dull the last time Sherriff had looked in. He would be quite different now. He would be gay and sparkling. He remembered two good stories he would like to tell Sherriff.

The door opened and Claire came in. There was a silence. She stood looking at him in a way that puzzled Mr Pickering. If it had not been for her attitude at their last meeting and the manner in which she had broken that last meeting up, he would have said that her look seemed somehow to strike a note of appeal. There was something soft and repentant about her. She suggested, it seemed to Mr Pickering, the prodigal daughter revisiting the old homestead.

'Dudley!'

She smiled a faint smile, a wistful, deprecating smile. She was looking lovelier than ever. Her face glowed with a wonderful colour and her eyes were very bright. Mr Pickering met her gaze, and strange things began to happen to his mind, that mind which a moment before had thought so clearly and established so definite a point of view.

What a gelatine-backboned thing is man, who prides himself on his clear reason and becomes as wet blotting-paper at one glance from bright eyes! A moment before Mr Pickering had thought out the whole subject of woman and marriage in a few bold flashes of his capable brain, and thanked Providence that he was not as those men who take unto themselves wives to their undoing. Now in an instant he had lost that iron outlook. Reason was temporarily out of business. He was slipping.

'Dudley!'

For a space Subconscious Self thrust itself forward.

'Look out! Be careful!' it warned.

Mr Pickering ignored it. He was watching, fascinated, the glow on Claire's face, her shining eyes.

'Dudley, I want to speak to you.'

'Tell her you can only be seen by appointment! Escape! Bolt!'

Mr Pickering did not bolt. Claire came towards him, still smiling that pathetic smile. A thrill permeated Mr Pickering's entire one hundred and ninety-seven pounds, trickling down his spine like hot water and coming out at the soles of his feet. He had forgotten now that he had ever sneered at marriage. It seemed to him now that there was nothing in life to be compared with that beatific state, and that bachelors were mere wild asses of the desert.

Claire came and sat down on the arm of his chair He moved convulsively, but he stayed where he was.

'Fool!' said Subconscious Self.

Claire took hold of his hand and patted it. He quivered, but remained.

'Ass!' hissed Subconscious Self.

Claire stopped patting his hand and began to stroke it. Mr Pickering breathed heavily.

'Dudley, dear,' said Claire, softly, 'I've been an awful fool, and I'm dreadful, dreadful sorry, and you're going to be the nicest, kindest, sweetest man on earth and tell me you've forgiven me. Aren't you?'

Mr Pickering's lips moved silently. Claire kissed the thinning summit of his head. There was a pause.

'Where is it?' she asked.

Mr Pickering started.

'Eh?'

'Where is it? Where did you put it? The ring, silly!'

Mr Pickering became aware that Subconscious Self was

addressing him. The occasion was tense, and Subconscious Self did not mince its words.

'You poor, maudlin, sentimental, doddering chunk of imbecility,' it said; 'are there no limits to your insanity? After all I said to you just now, are you deliberately going to start the old idiocy all over again?'

'She's so beautiful!' pleaded Mr Pickering. 'Look at her eyes!'

'Ass! Don't you remember what I said about beauty?'

'Yes, I know, but –'

'She's as hard as nails.'

'I'm sure you're wrong.'

'I'm not wrong.'

'But she loves me.'

'Forget it!'

Claire jogged his shoulders.

'Dudley, dear, what are you sitting there dreaming for? Where did you put the ring?'

Mr Pickering fumbled for it, located it, produced it. Claire examined it fondly.

'Did she throw it at him and nearly break his heart!' she said.

'Bolt!' urged Subconscious Self. 'Fly! Go to Japan!'

Mr Pickering did not go to Japan. He was staring worshippingly at Claire. With rapturous gaze he noted the grey glory of her eyes, the delicate curve of her cheek, the grace of her neck. He had no time to listen to pessimistic warnings from any Gloomy Gus of a Subconscious Self. He was ashamed that he had ever even for a moment allowed himself to be persuaded that Claire was not all that was perfect. No more doubts and hesitations for Dudley Pickering. He was under the influence.

'There!' said Claire, and slipped the ring on her finger.

She kissed the top of his head once more.

'So there we are!' she said.

'There we are!' gurgled the infatuated Dudley.

'Happy now?'

'Ur-r!'

'Then kiss me.'

Mr Pickering kissed her.

'Dudley, darling,' said Claire, 'we're going to be awfully, awfully happy, aren't we?'

'You bet we are!' said Mr Pickering.

Subconscious Self said nothing, being beyond speech.

21

FOR some minutes after Claire had left him Bill remained where he was, motionless. He felt physically incapable of moving. All the strength that was in him he was using to throw off the insidious poison of her parting speech, and it became plainer to him with each succeeding moment that he would have need of strength.

It is part of the general irony of things that in life's crises a man's good qualities are often the ones that help him least, if indeed they do not actually turn treacherously and fight against him. It was so with Bill. Modesty, if one may trust to the verdict of the mass of mankind, is a good quality. It sweetens the soul and makes for a kindly understanding of one's fellows. But arrogance would have served Bill better now. It was his fatal habit of self-depreciation that was making Claire's words so specious as he stood there trying to cast them from his mind. Who was he, after all, that he should imagine that he had won on his personal merits a girl like Elizabeth Boyd?

He had the not very common type of mind that perceives the merit in others more readily than their faults, and in himself the faults more readily than the merit. Time and the society of a great number of men of different ranks and natures had rid him of the outer symbol of this type of mind, which is shyness, but it had left him still unconvinced that he amounted to anything very much as an individual.

This was the thought that met him every time he tried to persuade himself that what Claire had said was ridiculous, the mere parting shaft of an angry woman. With this thought as an ally her words took on a plausibility hard to withstand. Plausible! That was the devil of it. By no effort could he blind himself to the fact that they were that. In the light of Claire's insinuations what had seemed coincidences took on a more sinister character. It had seemed to him an odd and lucky chance that Nutty Boyd should have come to the rooms which he was occupying that night, seeking a companion. Had it been chance? Even at the time he had thought it strange that, on the strength of a single evening spent together, Nutty should have invited a total stranger to make an indefinite visit to his home. Had there been design behind the invitation?

Bill began to walk slowly to the house. He felt tired and unhappy. He meant to go to bed and try to sleep away these wretched doubts and questionings. Daylight would bring relief.

As he reached the open front door he caught the sound of voices, and paused for an instant, almost unconsciously, to place them. They came from one of the rooms upstairs. It was Nutty speaking now, and it was impossible for Bill not to hear what he said, for Nutty had abandoned his customary drawl in favour of a high, excited tone.

'Of course, you hate him and all that,' said Nutty; 'but after all you will be getting five million dollars that ought to have come to –'

That was all that Bill heard, for he had stumbled across the hall and was in his room, sitting on the bed and staring into the darkness with burning eyes. The door banged behind him.

So it was true!

There came a knock at the door. It was repeated. The handle turned.

'Is that you, Bill?'

It was Elizabeth's voice. He could just see her, framed in the doorway.

'Bill!'

His throat was dry. He swallowed, and found that he could speak.

'Yes?'

'Did you just come in?'

'Yes.'

'Then – you heard?'

'Yes.'

There was a long silence. Then the door closed gently and he heard her go upstairs.

22

WHEN Bill woke next morning it was ten o'clock; and his first emotion, on a day that was to be crowded with emotions of various kinds, was one of shame. The desire to do the fitting thing is innate in man, and it struck Bill, as he hurried through his toilet, that he must be a shallow, coarse-fibred sort of person, lacking in the finer feelings, not to have passed a sleepless night. There was something revolting in the thought that, in circumstances which would have made sleep an impossibility for most men, he had slept like a log. He did not do himself the justice to recollect that he had had a singularly strenuous day, and that it is Nature's business, which she performs quietly and unromantically, to send sleep to tired men regardless of their private feelings; and it was in a mood of dissatisfaction with the quality of his soul that he left his room.

He had a general feeling that he was not much of a chap and that when he died – which he trusted would be shortly – the world would be well rid of him. He felt humble and depressed and hopeless.

Elizabeth met him in the passage. At the age of eleven or thereabouts women acquire a poise and an ability to handle difficult situations which a man, if he is lucky, manages to achieve somewhere in the later seventies. Except for a pallor strange to her face and a drawn look about the eyes, there was nothing to show that all was not for the best with Elizabeth in a best of all possible worlds. If she did not look jaunty, she at least looked composed. She greeted Bill with a smile.

'I didn't wake you. I thought I would let you sleep on.'

The words had the effect of lending an additional clarity and firmness of outline to the picture of himself which Bill had already drawn in his mind – of a soulless creature sunk in hoggish slumber.

'We've had breakfast. Nutty has gone for a walk. Isn't he wonderful nowadays? I've kept your breakfast warm for you.'

Bill protested. He might be capable of sleep, but he was not going to sink to food.

'Not for me, thanks,' he said, hollowly.

'Come along.'

'Honestly –'

'Come along.'

He followed her meekly. How grimly practical women were! They let nothing interfere with the essentials of life. It seemed all wrong. Nevertheless, he breakfasted well and gratefully, Elizabeth watching him in silence across the table.

'Finished?'

'Yes, thanks.'

She hesitated for a moment.

'Well, Bill, I've slept on it. Things are in rather a muddle, aren't they? I think I had better begin by explaining what led up to those words you heard Nutty say last night. Won't you smoke?'

'No, thanks.'

'You'll feel better if you do.'

'I couldn't.'

A bee had flown in through the open window. She followed it with her eye as it blundered about the room. It flew out again into the sunshine. She turned to Bill again.

'They were supposed to be words of consolation,' she said.

Bill said nothing.

'Nutty, you see, has his own peculiar way of looking at things, and it didn't occur to him that I might have promised to marry you because I loved you. He took it for granted that I had done it to save the Boyd home. He has been very anxious from the first that I should marry you. I think that that must have been why he asked you down here. He found out in New York, you know, who you were. Someone you met at supper recognized you, and told Nutty. So, as far as that is concerned, the girl you were speaking to at the gate last night was right.'

He started. 'You heard her?'

'I couldn't help it. She meant me to hear. She was raising

her voice quite unnecessarily if she did not mean to include me in the conversation. I had gone in to find Nutty, and he was out, and I was coming back to you. That's how I was there. You didn't see me because your back was turned. She saw me.'

Bill met her eyes. 'You don't ask who she was?'

'It doesn't matter who she was. It's what she said that matters. She said that we knew you were Lord Dawlish.'

'Did you know?'

'Nutty told me two or three days ago.' Her voice shook and a flush came into her face. 'You probably won't believe it, but the news made absolutely no difference to me one way or the other. I had always imagined Lord Dawlish as a treacherous, adventurer sort of man, because I couldn't see how a man who was not like that could have persuaded Uncle Ira to leave him his money. But after knowing you even for this short time, I knew you were quite the opposite of that, and I remembered that the first thing you had done on coming into the money had been to offer me half, so the information that you were the Lord Dawlish whom I had been hating did not affect me. And the fact that you were rich and I was poor did not affect me either. I loved you, and that was all I cared about. If all this had not happened everything would have been all right. But, you see, nine-tenths of what that girl said to you was so perfectly true that it is humanly impossible for you not to believe the other tenth, which wasn't. And then, to clinch it, you hear Nutty consoling me. That brings me back to Nutty.'

'I –'

'Let me tell you about Nutty first. I said that he had always been anxious that I should marry you. Something happened last night to increase his anxiety. I have often wondered how he managed to get enough money to enable him to spend three days in New York, and last night he told me. He came in just after I had got back to the house after leaving you and that girl, and he was very scared. It seems that when the letter from the London lawyer came telling him that he had been left a hundred dollars, he got the idea of raising money on the strength of it. You know Nutty by this time, so you won't be surprised at the way he went about it. He borrowed a hundred dollars from the man at the chemist's on the security of that letter, and then – I suppose it seemed so easy that it struck him as a pity to let the opportunity slip – he did the same thing with four other tradesmen. Nutty's so odd that I don't know even now whether it ever occurred to him that he was obtaining money under false pretences; but the poor tradesmen hadn't any doubt about it at all. They compared notes and found what had happened, and last night, while we were in the woods, one of them came here and called Nutty a good many names and threatened him with imprisonment.

'You can imagine how delighted Nutty was when I came in and told him that I was engaged to you. In his curious way, he took it for granted that I had heard about his financial operations, and was doing it entirely for his sake, to get him out of his fix. And while I was trying to put him right on that point he began to console me. You see, Nutty looks on you as the enemy of the family, and it didn't strike him that it was possible that I didn't look on you in that light too. So, after being delighted for a while, he very sweetly thought that he ought to cheer me up and point out some of the compensations of marriage with you. And – Well, that was what you heard. There you have the full explanation. You can't possibly believe it.'

She broke off and began to drum her fingers on the table. And as she did so there came to Bill a sudden relief from all the doubts and black thoughts that had tortured him. Elizabeth was straight. Whatever appearances might seem to suggest, nothing could convince him that she was playing an underhand game. It was as if something evil had gone out of him. He felt lighter, cleaner. He could breathe.

'I do believe it,' he said. 'I believe every word you say.'

She shook her head.

'You can't in the face of the evidence.'

'I believe it.'

'No. You may persuade yourself for the moment that you do, but after a while you will have to go by the evidence. You won't be able to help yourself. You haven't realized what a crushing thing evidence is. You have to go by it against your will. You see, evidence is the only guide. You don't know that I am speaking the truth; you just feel it. You're trusting your heart and not your head. The head must win in the end. You might go on believing for a time, but sooner or later you would be bound to begin to doubt and worry and torment yourself. You couldn't fight against the evidence, when once your instinct – or whatever it is that tells you that I am speaking the truth – had begun to weaken. And it would weaken. Think what it would have to be fighting all the time. Think of the case your intelligence would be making out, day after day, till it crushed you. It's impossible that you could keep yourself from docketing the evidence and arranging it and absorbing it. Think! Consider what you know are actual facts! Nutty invites you down here, knowing that you are Lord Dawlish. All you know about my attitude towards Lord Dawlish is what I told you on the first morning of your visit. I told you I hated him. Yet, knowing you are Lord Dawlish, I become engaged to you. Directly afterwards you hear Nutty consoling me as if I were marrying you against my will. Isn't that an absolutely fair statement of what has happened? How could you go on believing me with all that against you?'

'I know you're straight. You couldn't do anything crooked.'

'The evidence proves that I did.'

'I don't care.'

'Not now.'

'Never.'

She shook her head.

'It's dear of you, Bill, but you're promising an impossibility. And just because it's impossible, and because I love you too much to face what would be bound to happen, I'm going to send you away.'

'Send me away!'

'Yes. It's going to hurt. You don't know how it's going to hurt, Bill; but it's the only thing to do. I love you too much to live with you for the rest of my life wondering all the time whether you still believed or whether the weight of the evidence had crushed out that tiny little spark of intuition which is all that makes you believe me now. You could never know the truth for certain, you see – that's the horror of it; and sometimes you would be able to make yourself believe, but more often, in spite of all you could do, you would doubt. It would poison both our lives. Little things would happen, insignificant in themselves, which would become tremendously important just because they added a little bit more to the doubt which you would never be able to get rid of.

'When we had quarrels – which we should, as we are both human – they wouldn't be over and done with in an hour. They would stick in your mind and rankle, because, you see, they might be proofs that I didn't really love you. And then when I seemed happy with you, you would wonder if I was acting. I know all this sounds morbid and exaggerated, but it isn't. What have you got to go on, as regards me? What do you really know of me? If something like this had happened after we had been married half a dozen years and really knew each other, we could laugh at it. But we are strangers. We came together and loved each other because there was something in each of us which attracted the other. We took that little something as a foundation and built on it. But what has happened has knocked away our poor little foundation. That's all. We don't really know anything at all about each other for certain. It's just guesswork.'

She broke off and looked at the clock.

'I had better be packing if you're to catch the train.'

He gave a rueful laugh.

'You're throwing me out!'

'Yes, I am. I want you to go while I am strong enough to let you go.'

'If you really feel like that, why send me away?'

'How do you know I really feel like that? How do you know that I am not pretending to feel like that as part of a carefully-prepared plan?'

He made an impatient gesture.

'Yes, I know,' she said. 'You think I am going out of my way to manufacture unnecessary complications. I'm not; I'm simply looking ahead. If I were trying to trap you for the sake of your money, could I play a stronger card than by seeming anxious to give you up? If I were to give in now, sooner or later that suspicion would come to you. You would drive it away. You might drive it away a hundred times. But you couldn't kill it. In the end it would beat you.'

He shrugged his shoulders helplessly.

'I can't argue.'

'Nor can I. I can only put very badly things which I know are true. Come and pack.'

'I'll do it. Don't you bother.'

'Nonsense! No man knows how to pack properly.'

He followed her to his room, pulled out his suitcase, the symbol of the end of all things, watched her as she flitted about, the sun shining on her hair as she passed and repassed the window. She was picking things up, folding them, packing them. Bill looked on with an aching sense of desolation. It was all so friendly, so intimate, so exactly as it would have been if she were his wife. It seemed to him needlessly cruel that she should be playing on this note of domesticity at the moment when she was barring for ever the door between him and happiness. He rebelled helplessly against the attitude she had taken. He had not thought it all out, as she had done. It was folly, insanity, ruining their two lives like this for a scruple.

Once again he was to encounter that practical strain in the feminine mind which jars upon a man in trouble. She was holding something in her hand and looking at it with concern.

'Why didn't you tell me?' she said. 'Your socks are in an awful state, poor boy!'

He had the feeling of having been hit by something. A man has not a woman's gift of being able to transfer his mind at will from sorrow to socks.

'Like sieves!' She sighed. A troubled frown wrinkled her forehead. 'Men are so helpless! Oh, dear, I'm sure you don't pay any attention to anything important. I don't believe you ever bother your head about keeping warm in winter and not getting your feet wet. And now I shan't be able to look after you!'

Bill's voice broke. He felt himself trembling.

'Elizabeth!'

She was kneeling on the floor, her head bent over the suit-case. She looked up and met his eyes.

'It's no use, Bill, dear. I must. It's the only way.'

The sense of the nearness of the end broke down the numbness which held him.

'Elizabeth! It's so utterly absurd. It's just – chucking everything away!'

She was silent for a moment.

'Bill, dear, I haven't said anything about it before but don't you see that there's my side to be considered too? I only showed you that you could never possibly know that I loved you. How am I to know that you really love me?'

He had moved a step towards her. He drew back, chilled.

'I can't do more than tell you,' he said.

'You can't. And there you have put in two words just what I've been trying to make clear all the time. Don't you see that that's the terrible thing about life; that nobody can do more than tell anybody anything? Life's nothing but words, words, words; and how are we to know when words are true? How am I to know that you didn't ask me to marry you out of sheer pity and an exaggerated sense of justice?'

He stared at her.

'That,' he said, 'is absolutely ridiculous!'

'Why? Look at it as I should look at it later on, when whatever it is inside me that tells me it's ridiculous now had died. Just at this moment, while we're talking here, there's something stronger than reason which tells me you really do love me. But can't you understand that that won't last? It's like a candle burning on a rock with the tide coming up all round it. It's burning brightly enough now, and we can see the truth by the light of it. But the tide will put it out, and then we shall have nothing left to see by. There's a great black sea of suspicion and doubt creeping up to swamp the little spark of intuition inside us.

'I will tell you what would happen to me if I didn't send you away. Remember I heard what that girl was saying last night. Remember that you hated the thought of depriving me of

Uncle Ira's money so much that your first act was to try to get me to accept half of it. The quixotic thing is the first that it occurs to you to do, because you're like that, because you're the straightest, whitest man I've ever known or shall know. Could anything be more likely, looking at it as I should later on, than that you should have hit on the idea of marrying me as the only way of undoing the wrong you thought you had done me? I've been foolish about obligations all my life. I've a sort of morbid pride that hates the thought of owing anything to anybody, of getting anything that I have not earned. By and by, if I were to marry you, a little rotten speck of doubt would begin to eat its way farther and farther into me. It would be the same with you. We should react on each other. We should be watching each other, testing each other, trying each other out all the time. It would be horrible, horrible!'

He started to speak; then, borne down by the hopelessness of it, stopped. Elizabeth stood up. They did not look at each other. He strapped the suitcase and picked it up. The end of all things was at hand.

'Better to end it all cleanly, Bill,' she said, in a low voice. 'It will hurt less.'

He did not speak.

'I'll come down to the gate with you.'

They walked in silence down the drive. The air was heavy with contentment. He hummed a tune.

'Good-bye, Bill, dear.'

He took her hand dully.

'Good-bye,' he said.

Elizabeth stood at the gate, watching. He swung down the road with long strides. At the bend he turned and for a moment stood there, as if waiting for her to make some sign. Then he fell into his stride again and was gone. Elizabeth leaned on the gate. Her face was twisted, and she clutched the warm wood as if it gave her strength.

The grounds were very empty. The spirit of loneliness brooded on them. Elizabeth walked slowly back to the house. Nutty was coming towards her from the orchard.

'Halloa!' said Nutty.

He was cheerful and debonair. His little eyes were alight with contentment. He hummed a tune.

'Where's Dawlish?' he said.

'He has gone.'

Nutty's tune failed in the middle of a bar. Something in his sister's voice startled him. The glow of contentment gave way to a look of alarm.

'Gone? How do you mean – gone? You don't mean – gone?'

'Yes.'

'Gone away?'

'Gone away.'

They had reached the house before he spoke again.

'You don't mean – gone away?'

'Yes.'

'Do you mean – gone away?'

'Yes.'

'You aren't going to marry him?'

'No.'

The world stood still. The noise of the crickets and all the little sounds of summer smote on Nutty's ear in one discordant shriek.

'Oh, gosh!' he exclaimed, faintly, and collapsed on the front steps like a jelly-fish.

23

THE spectacle of Nutty in his anguish did not touch Elizabeth. Normally a kind-hearted girl, she was not in the least sorry for him. She had even taken a bitter pleasure and found a momentary relief in loosing the thunderbolt which had smitten him down. Even if it has to manufacture it, misery loves company. She watched Nutty with a cold and uninterested eye as he opened his mouth feebly, shut it again and reopened it; and then when it became apparent that these manoeuvres were about to result in speech, she left him and walked quickly down the drive again. She had the feeling that if Nutty were to begin to ask her questions – and he had the aspect of one who is about to ask a thousand – she would break down. She wanted solitude and movement, so she left Nutty sitting and started for the gate. Presently she would go and do things among the bee-hives; and after that, if that brought no solace, she would go in and turn the house upside down and get dusty and tired. Anything to occupy herself.

Reaction had set in. She had known it would come, and had made ready to fight against it, but she had underestimated the strength of the enemy. It seemed to her, in those first minutes, that she had done a mad thing; that all those arguments which she had used were far-fetched and ridiculous. It was useless to tell herself that she had thought the whole thing out clearly and had taken the only course that could have been taken. With Bill's departure the power to face the situation steadily had left her. All she could think of was that she loved him and that she had sent him away.

Why had he listened to her? Why hadn't he taken her in his arms and told her not to be a little fool? Why did men ever listen to women? If he had really loved her, would he have gone away? She tormented herself with this last question for a while. She was still tormenting herself with it when a melancholy voice broke in on her meditations.

'I can't believe it,' said the voice. She turned, to perceive Nutty drooping beside her. 'I simply can't believe it!'

Elizabeth clenched her teeth. She was not in the mood for Nutty.

'It will gradually sink in,' she said, unsympathetically.

'Did you really send him away?'

'I did.'

'But what on earth for?'

'Because it was the only thing to do.'

A light shone on Nutty's darkness.

'Oh, I say, did he hear what I said last night?'

'He did hear what you said last night.'

Nutty's mouth opened slowly.

'Oh!'

Elizabeth said nothing.

'But you could have explained that.'

'How?'

'Oh, I don't know – somehow or other.' He appeared to think. 'But you said it was you who sent him away.'

'I did.'

'Well, this beats me!'

Elizabeth's strained patience reached the limit.

'Nutty, please!' she said. 'Don't let's talk about it. It's all over now.'

'Yes, but –'

'Nutty, don't! I can't stand it. I'm raw all over. I'm hating myself. Please don't make it worse.'

Nutty looked at her face, and decided not to make it worse. But his anguish demanded some outlet. He found it in soliloquy.

'Just like this for the rest of our lives!' he murmured, taking in the farm-grounds and all that in them stood with one glassy stare of misery. 'Nothing but ghastly bees and sweeping floors and fetching water till we die of old age! That is, if those blighters don't put me in jail for getting that money out of them. How was I to know that it was obtaining money under false pretences? It simply seemed to me a darned good way of collecting a few dollars. I don't see how I'm ever going to pay them back, so I suppose it's prison for me all right.'

Elizabeth had been trying not to listen to him, but without success.

'I'll look after that, Nutty. I have a little money saved up, enough to pay off what you owe. I was saving it for something else, but never mind.'

'Awfully good of you,' said Nutty, but his voice sounded almost disappointed. He was in the frame of mind which resents alleviation of its gloom. He would have preferred at that moment to be allowed to round off the picture of the future which he was constructing in his mind with a reel or two showing himself brooding in a cell. After all, what difference did it make to a man of spacious tastes whether he languished for the rest of his life in a jail or on a farm in the country? Jail, indeed, was almost preferable. You knew where you were when you were in prison. They didn't spring things on you.

Whereas life on a farm was nothing but one long succession of things sprung on you. Now that Lord Dawlish had gone, he supposed that Elizabeth would make him help her with the bees again. At this thought he groaned aloud. When he contemplated a lifetime at Flack's, a lifetime of bee-dodging and carpet-beating and water-lugging, and reflected that, but for a few innocent words – words spoken, mark you, in a pure spirit of kindliness and brotherly love with the object of putting a bit of optimistic pep into sister! – he might have been in a position to touch a millionaire brother-in-law for the needful whenever he felt disposed, the iron entered into Nutty's soul. A rotten, rotten world!

Nutty had the sort of mind that moves in circles. After contemplating for a time the rottenness of the world, he came back to the point from which he had started.

'I can't understand it,' he said. 'I can't believe it.'

He kicked a small pebble that lay convenient to his foot.

'You say you sent him away. If he had legged it on his own account, because of what he heard me say, I could understand that. But why should you –'

It became evident to Elizabeth that, until some explanation of this point was offered to him, Nutty would drift about in her vicinity, moaning and shuffling his feet indefinitely.

'I sent him away because I loved him,' she said, 'and because, after what had happened, he could never be certain that I loved him. Can you understand that?'

'No,' said Nutty, frankly, 'I'm darned if I can! It sounds loony to me.'

'You can't see that it wouldn't have been fair to him to marry him?'

'No.'

The doubts which she was trying to crush increased the violence of their attack. It was not that she respected Nutty's judgement in itself. It was that his view of what she had done chimed in so neatly with her own. She longed for someone to tell her that she had done right: someone who would bring back that feeling of certainty which she had had during her talk with Bill. And in these circumstances Nutty's attitude had more weight than on its merits it deserved. She wished she could cry. She had a feeling that if she once did that the right outlook would come back to her.

Nutty, meanwhile, had found another pebble and was kicking it sombrely. He was beginning to perceive something of the intricate and unfathomable workings of the feminine mind. He had always looked on Elizabeth as an ordinary good fellow, a girl whose mind worked in a more or less understandable way. She was not one of those hysterical women you read about in the works of the novelists; she was just a regular girl. And yet now, at the one moment of her life when everything depended on her acting sensibly, she had behaved in a way that made his head swim when he thought of it. What it amounted to was that you simply couldn't understand women.

Into this tangle of silent sorrow came a hooting automobile. It drew up at the gate and a man jumped out.

24

THE man who had alighted from the automobile was young and cheerful. He wore a flannel suit of a gay blue and a straw hat with a coloured ribbon, and he looked upon a world which, his manner seemed to indicate, had been constructed according to his own specifications through a single eyeglass. When he spoke it became plain that his nationality was English.

Nutty regarded his beaming countenance with a lowering hostility. The indecency of anyone being cheerful at such a time struck him forcibly. He would have liked mankind to have preserved till further notice a hushed gloom. He glared at the young man.

Elizabeth, such was her absorption in her thoughts, was not even aware of his presence till he spoke to her.

'I beg your pardon, is this Flack's?'

She looked up and met that sunny eyeglass.

'This is Flack's,' she said.

'Thank you,' said the young man.

The automobile, a stout, silent man at the helm, throbbed in the nervous way automobiles have when standing still, suggesting somehow that it were best to talk quick, as they can give you only a few minutes before dashing on to keep some other appointment. Either this or a natural volatility lent a breezy rapidity to the visitor's speech. He looked at Elizabeth across the gate, which it had not occured to her to open, as if she were just what he had expected her to be and a delight to his eyes, and burst into speech.

'My name's Nichols – J. Nichols. I expect you remember getting a letter from me a week or two ago?'

The name struck Elizabeth as familiar. But he had gone on to identify himself before she could place it in her mind.

'Lawyer, don't you know. Wrote you a letter telling you that your Uncle Ira Nutcombe had left all his money to Lord Dawlish.'

'Oh, yes,' said Elizabeth, and was about to invite him to pass the barrier, when he began to speak again.

'You know, I want to explain that letter. Wrote it on a sudden impulse, don't you know. The more I have to do with the law, the more it seems to hit me that a lawyer oughtn't to act on impulse. At the moment, you see, it seemed to me the decent thing to do – put you out of your misery, and so forth – stop your entertaining hopes never to be realized, what? and all that sort of thing. You see, it was like this: Bill – I mean Lord Dawlish – is a great pal of mine, a dear old chap. You ought to know him. Well, being in the know, you understand, through your uncle having deposited the will with us, I gave Bill the tip directly I heard of Mr Nutcombe's death. I sent him a telephone message to come to the office, and I said: "Bill, old man, this old buster" – I beg your pardon, this old gentleman – "has left you all his money." Quite informal, don't you know, and at the same time, in the same informal spirit, I wrote you the letter.' He dammed the torrent for a moment. 'By the way, of course you are Miss Elizabeth Boyd, what?'

'Yes.'

The young man seemed relieved.

'I'm glad of that,' he said. 'Funny if you hadn't been. You'd have wondered what on earth I was talking about.'

In spite of her identity, this was precisely what Elizabeth was doing. Her mind, still under a cloud, had been unable to understand one word of Mr Nichols's discourse. Judging from his appearance, which was that of a bewildered hosepipe or a snake whose brain is being momentarily overtaxed, Nutty was in the same difficulty. He had joined the group at the gate, abandoning the pebble which he had been kicking in the background, and was now leaning on the top bar, a picture of silent perplexity.

'You see, the trouble is,' resumed the young man, 'my governor, who's the head of the firm, is all for doing things according to precedent. He loves red tape – wears it wrapped round him in winter instead of flannel. He's all for doing things in the proper legal way, which, as I dare say you know, takes months. And, meanwhile, everybody's wondering what's happening and who has got the money, and so on and so forth. I thought I would skip all that and let you know right away exactly where you stood, so I wrote you that letter. I don't think my temperament's quite suited to the law, don't you know, and if he ever hears that I wrote you that letter I have a notion that the governor will think so too. So I came over here to ask you, if you don't mind, not to mention it when you get in touch with the governor. I frankly admit that that letter, written with the best intentions, was a bloomer.'

With which manly admission the young man paused, and allowed the rays of his eyeglass to play upon Elizabeth in silence. Elizabeth tried to piece together what little she understood of his monologue.

'You mean that you want me not to tell your father that I got a letter from you?'

'Exactly that. And thanks very much for not saying "without prejudice," or anything of that kind. The governor would have.'

'But I don't understand. Why should you think that I should ever mention anything to your father?'

'Might slip out, you know, without your meaning it.'

'But when? I shall never meet your father.'

'You might quite easily. He might want to see you about the money.'

'The money?'

The eyebrow above the eyeglass rose, surprised.

'Haven't you had a letter from the governor?'

'No.'

The young man made a despairing gesture.

'I took it for granted that it had come on the same boat that I did. There you have the governor's methods! Couldn't want a better example. I suppose some legal formality or other has cropped up and laid him a stymie, and he's waiting to get round it. You really mean he hasn't written?

'Why, dash it,' said the young man, as one to whom all is revealed, 'then you can't have understood a word of what I've been saying!'

For the first time Elizabeth found herself capable of smiling. She liked this incoherent young man.

'I haven't,' she said.

'You don't know about the will?'

'Only what you told me in your letter.'

'Well, I'm hanged! Tell me – I hadn't the honour of knowing him personally – was the late Mr Nutcombe's whole life as eccentric as his will-making? It seems to me –'

Nutty spoke.

'Uncle Ira's middle name,' he said, 'was Bloomingdale. That,' he proceeded, bitterly, 'is the frightful injustice of it all. I had to suffer from it right along, and all I get, when it comes to a finish, is a miserable hundred dollars. Uncle Ira insisted on father and mother calling me Nutcombe; and whenever he got a new craze I was always the one he worked it off on. You remember the time he became a vegetarian, Elizabeth? Gosh!' Nutty brooded coldly on the past. 'You remember the time he had it all worked out that the end of the world was to come at five in the morning one February? Made me stop up all night with him, reading Marcus Aurelius! And the steam-heat turned off at twelve-thirty! I could tell you a dozen things just as bad as that. He always picked on me. And now I've gone through it all he leaves me a hundred dollars!'

Mr Nichols nodded sympathetically.

'I should have imagined that he was rather like that. You know, of course, why he made that will I wrote to you about, leaving all his money to Bill Dawlish? Simply because Bill, who met him golfing at a place in Cornwall in the off season, cured him of slicing his approach-shots! I give you my word that was the only reason. I'm sorry for old Bill, poor old chap. Such a good sort!'

'He's all right,' said Nutty. 'But why you should be sorry for him gets past me. A fellow who gets five million –'

'But he doesn't, don't you see?'

'How do you mean?'

'Why, this other will puts him out of the running.'

'Which other will?'

'Why, the one I'm telling you about.'

He looked from one to the other, apparently astonished at their slowness of understanding. Then an idea occurred to him.

'Why, now that I think of it, I never told you, did I? Yes, your uncle made another will at the very last moment, leaving all he possessed to Miss Boyd.'

The dead silence in which his words were received stimulated him to further speech. It occurred to him that, after that letter of his, perhaps these people were wary about believing anything he said.

'It's absolutely true. It's the real, stable information this time. I had it direct from the governor, who was there when he made the will. He and the governor had had a row about something, you know, and they made it up during those last days, and – Well, apparently your uncle thought he had better celebrate it somehow, so he made a new will. From what little I know of him, that was the way he celebrated most things. I took it for granted the governor would have written to you by this time. I expect you'll hear by the next mail. You see, what brought me over was the idea that when he wrote you might possibly take it into your heads to mention having heard from me. You don't know my governor. If he found out I had done that I should never hear the last of it. So I said to him: "Gov'nor, I'm feeling a bit jaded. Been working too hard, or something. I'll take a week or so off, if you can spare me." He didn't object, so I whizzed over. Well, of course, I'm awfully sorry for old Bill, but I congratulate you, Miss Boyd.'

'What's the time?' said Elizabeth.

Mr Nichols was surprised. He could not detect the connexion of ideas.

'It's about five to eleven,' he said, consulting his watch.

The next moment he was even more surprised, for Elizabeth, making nothing of the barrier of the gate, had rushed past him and was even now climbing into his automobile.

'Take me to the station, at once,' she was crying to the stout, silent man, whom not even these surprising happenings had shaken from his attitude of well-fed detachment.

The stout man, ceasing to be silent, became interrogative.

'Uh?'

'Take me to the station. I must catch the eleven o'clock train.'

The stout man was not a rapid thinker. He enveloped her in a stodgy gaze. It was only too plain to Elizabeth that he was a man who liked to digest one idea slowly before going on to absorb the next. Jerry Nichols had told him to drive to Flack's. He had driven to Flack's. Here he was at Flack's. Now this young woman was telling him to drive to the station. It was a new idea, and he bent himself to the Fletcherizing of it.

'I'll give you ten dollars if you get me there by eleven,' shouted Elizabeth.

The car started as if it were some living thing that had had a sharp instrument jabbed into it. Once or twice in his life it had happened to the stout man to encounter an idea which he could swallow at a gulp. This was one of them.

Mr Nichols, following the car with a wondering eye, found that Nutty was addressing him.

'Is this really true?' said Nutty.

'Absolute gospel.'

A wild cry, a piercing whoop of pure joy, broke the summer stillness.

'Come and have a drink, old man!' babbled Nutty. 'This

wants celebrating!' His face fell. 'Oh, I was forgetting! I'm on the wagon.'

'On the wagon?'

'Sworn off, you know. I'm never going to touch another drop as long as I live. I began to see things – monkeys!'

'I had a pal,' said Mr Nichols, sympathetically, 'who used to see kangaroos.'

Nutty seized him by the arm, hospitable though handicapped.

'Come and have a bit of bread and butter, or a slice of cake or something, and a glass of water. I want to tell you a lot more about Uncle Ira, and I want to hear all about your end of it. Gee, what a day!'

' "The maddest, merriest of all the glad New Year," ' assented Mr Nichols. 'A slice of that old 'eighty-seven cake. Just the thing!'

25

BILL made his way along the swaying train to the smoking-car, which was almost empty. It had come upon him overwhelmingly that he needed tobacco. He was in the mood when a man must either smoke or give up altogether the struggle with Fate. He lit his pipe, and looked out of the window at Long Island racing past him. It was only a blur to him.

The conductor was asking for tickets. Bill showed his mechanically, and the conductor passed on. Then he settled down once more to his thoughts. He could not think coherently yet. His walk to the station had been like a walk in a dream. He was conscious of a great, dull pain that weighed on his mind, smothering it. The trees and houses still moved past him in the same indistinguishable blur.

He became aware that the conductor was standing beside him, saying something about a ticket. He produced his once more, but this did not seem to satisfy the conductor. To get rid of the man, who was becoming a nuisance, he gave him his whole attention, as far as that smothering weight would allow him to give his whole attention to anything, and found that the man was saying strange things. He thought that he could not have heard him correctly.

'What?' he said.

'Lady back there told me to collect her fare from you,' repeated the conductor. 'Said you would pay.'

Bill blinked. Either there was some mistake or trouble had turned his brain. He pushed himself together with a supreme effort.

'A lady said I would pay her fare?'

'Yes.'

'But – but why?' demanded Bill, feebly.

The conductor seemed unwilling to go into first causes.

'Search me!' he replied.

'Pay her fare!'

'Told me to collect it off the gentleman in the grey suit in the smoking-car. You're the only one that's got a grey suit.'

'There's some mistake.'

'Not mine.'

'What does she look like?'

The conductor delved in his mind for adjectives.

'Small,' he said, collecting them slowly. 'Brown eyes –'

He desisted from his cataloguing at this point, for, with a loud exclamation, Bill had dashed away.

Two cars farther back he had dropped into the seat by Elizabeth and was gurgling wordlessly. A massive lady, who had entered the train at East Moriches in company with three children and a cat in a basket, eyed him with a curiosity that she made no attempt to conceal. Two girls in a neighbouring seat leaned forward eagerly to hear all. This was because one of them had told the other that Elizabeth was Mary Pickford. Her companion was sceptical, but nevertheless obviously impressed.

'My God!' said Bill.

The massive lady told the three children sharply to look at their picture-book.

'Well, I'm hanged!'

The mother of three said that if her offspring did not go right along to the end of the car and look at the pretty trees trouble must infallibly ensue.

'Elizabeth!'

At the sound of the name the two girls leaned back, taking no further interest in the proceedings.

'What are you doing here?'

Elizabeth smiled, a shaky but encouraging smile.

'I came after you, Bill.'

'You've got no hat!'

'I was in too much of a hurry to get one, and I gave all my money to the man who drove the car. That's why I had to ask you to pay my fare. You see, I'm not too proud to use your money after all.'

'Then –'

'Tickets please. One seventy-nine.'

It was the indefatigable conductor, sensible of his duty to the company and resolved that nothing should stand in the way of its performance. Bill gave him five dollars and told him to keep the change. The conductor saw eye to eye with him in this.

'Bill! You gave him – ' She gave a little shrug of her shoulders. 'Well, it's lucky you're going to marry a rich girl.'

A look of the utmost determination overspread Bill's face.

'I don't know what you're talking about. I'm going to marry you. Now that I've got you again I'm not going to let you go. You can use all the arguments you like, but it won't matter. I was a fool ever to listen. If you try the same sort of thing again I'm just going to pick you up and carry you off. I've been thinking it over since I left you. My mind has been working absolutely clearly. I've gone into the whole thing. It's perfect rot to take the attitude you did. We know we love each other, and I'm not going to listen to any talk about time making us doubt it. Time will only make us love each other all the more.'

'Why, Bill, this is eloquence.'

'I feel eloquent.'

The stout lady ceased to listen. They had lowered their voices and she was hard of hearing. She consoled herself by taking up her copy of Gingery Stories and burying herself in the hectic adventures of a young millionaire and an artist's model.

Elizabeth caught a fleeting glimpse of the cover.

'I bet there's a story in there of a man named Harold who

188

was too proud to marry a girl, though he loved her, because she was rich and he wasn't. You wouldn't be so silly as that, Bill, would you?'

'It's the other way about with me.'

'No, it's not. Bill, do you know a man named Nichols?'

'Nichols?'

'J. Nichols. He said he knew you. He said he had told you about Uncle Ira leaving you his money.'

'Jerry Nichols! How on earth – Oh, I remember. He wrote to you, didn't he?'

'He did. And this morning, just after you had left, he called.'

'Jerry Nichols called?'

'To tell me that Uncle Ira had made another will before he died, leaving the money to me.'

Their eyes met.

'So I stole his car and caught the train,' said Elizabeth, simply.

Bill was recovering slowly from the news.

'But – this makes rather a difference, you know,' he said.

'In what way?'

'Well, what I mean to say is, you've got five million dollars and I've got two thousand a year, don't you know, and so –'

Elizabeth tapped him on the knee.

'Bill, do you see what this is in my hand?'

'Eh? What?'

'It's a pin. And I'm going to dig it right into you wherever I think it will hurt most, unless you stop being Harold at once. I'll tell you exactly what you've got to do, and you needn't think you're going to do anything else. When we get to New York, I first borrow the money from you to buy a hat, and then we walk to the City Hall, where you go to the window marked "Marriage Licences", and buy one. It will cost you one dollar. You will give your correct name and age and you will hear mine. It will come as a shock to you to know that my second name is something awful! I've kept it concealed all my life. After we've done that we shall go to the only church that anybody could possibly be married in. It's on Twenty-ninth Street, just round the corner from Fifth Avenue. It's got a fountain playing in front of it, and it's a little bit of heaven dumped right down in the middle of New York. And after that – well, we might start looking about for that farm we've talked of. We can get a good farm for five million dollars, and leave something over to be doled out – cautiously – to Nutty.

'And then all we have to do is to live happily ever after.'

Something small and soft slipped itself into his hand, just as it had done ages and ages ago in Lady Wetherby's wood.

It stimulated Bill's conscience to one last remonstrance.

'But, I say, you know –'

'Well?'

'This business of the money, you know. What I mean to say is – Ow!'

He broke off, as a sharp pain manifested itself in the fleshy part of his leg. Elizabeth was looking at him reprovingly, her weapon poised for another onslaught.

'I told you!' she said.

'All right, I won't do it again.'

'That's a good child. Bill, listen. Come closer and tell me all sorts of nice things about myself till we get to Jamaica, and then I'll tell you what I think of you. We've just passed Islip, so you've plenty of time.'

FOR THE BEST IN PAPERBACKS, LOOK FOR THE 🐧

In every corner of the world, on every subject under the sun, Penguin represents quality and variety – the very best in publishing today.

For complete information about books available from Penguin – including Puffins, Penguin Classics and Arkana – and how to order them, write to us at the appropriate address below. Please note that for copyright reasons the selection of books varies from country to country.

In the United Kingdom: Please write to *Dept E.P., Penguin Books Ltd, Harmondsworth, Middlesex, UB7 0DA.*

If you have any difficulty in obtaining a title, please send your order with the correct money, plus ten per cent for postage and packaging, to *PO Box No 11, West Drayton, Middlesex*

In the United States: Please write to *Dept BA, Penguin, 299 Murray Hill Parkway, East Rutherford, New Jersey 07073*

In Canada: Please write to *Penguin Books Canada Ltd, 2801 John Street, Markham, Ontario L3R 1B4*

In Australia: Please write to the *Marketing Department, Penguin Books Australia Ltd, P.O. Box 257, Ringwood, Victoria 3134*

In New Zealand: Please write to the *Marketing Department, Penguin Books (NZ) Ltd, Private Bag, Takapuna, Auckland 9*

In India: Please write to *Penguin Overseas Ltd, 706 Eros Apartments, 56 Nehru Place, New Delhi, 110019*

In the Netherlands: Please write to *Penguin Books Netherlands B.V., Postbus 195, NL–1380AD Weesp*

In West Germany: Please write to *Penguin Books Ltd, Friedrichstrasse 10–12, D–6000 Frankfurt/Main 1*

In Spain: Please write to *Longman Penguin España, Calle San Nicolas 15, E–28013 Madrid*

In Italy: Please write to *Penguin Italia s.r.l., Via Como 4, I-20096 Pioltello (Milano)*

In France: Please write to *Penguin Books Ltd, 39 Rue de Montmorency, F–75003 Paris*

In Japan: Please write to *Longman Penguin Japan Co Ltd, Yamaguchi Building, 2–12–9 Kanda Jimbocho, Chiyoda-Ku, Tokyo 101*

BY THE SAME AUTHOR

Life at Blandings

**Full Moon   Galahad at Blandings   Heavy Weather
A Pelican at Blandings   Pigs Have Wings
Service with a Smile   Something Fresh
Summer Lightning   Sunset at Blandings
Uncle Fred in the Springtime**
and the omnibus
Life at Blandings

Short Stories

**Blandings Castle   Lord Emsworth and Others
Eggs, Beans and Crumpets   The Man with Two Left Feet
The Man Upstairs and Other Stories
The Gold Bat and Other School Stories
The Pothunters and Other School Stories**

The Mike and Psmith Books

**Mike at Wrykyn   Mike and Psmith
Leave it to Psmith   Psmith in the City   Psmith, Journalist**

and

**The Adventures of Sally   Aunts Aren't Gentlemen
Bachelors Anonymous   Big Money   Cocktail Time
Company for Henry   A Damsel in Distress
Do Butlers Burgle Banks?   Doctor Sally
A Gentleman of Leisure   The Girl in Blue
Hot Water   The Indiscretions of Archie   Laughing Gas
The Little Nugget   The Luck of the Bodkins   Meet Mr Mulliner
Money in the Bank   Pearls, Girls and Monty Bodkin
Piccadilly Jim   Quick Service   Sam the Sudden
The Small Bachelor   Spring Fever   Summer Moonshine
Ukridge   Uncle Dynamite   Uneasy Money
Young Men in Spats**